Living Language Living Memory

Essays on the Works of Toni Morrison

Edited by   Kerstin W Shands
                 Giulia Grillo Mikrut

ENGLISH STUDIES 4

Södertörns högskola 2014

Cover photo: Hobcaw Barony, South Carolina,
by Kerstin W. Shands
Cover design: Jonathan Robson
Layout: Per Lindblom & Jonathan Robson

First published in 2014
Printed in Sweden by Elanders

English Studies 4
ISSN: 1651-4165

ISBN: 978-91-86069-95-7

Contents

Introduction

In 1993 Toni Morrison was awarded the Nobel Prize for Literature. On awarding the prize the Nobel committee described her work as "characterized by visionary force and poetic import [that] gives life to an essential aspect of American reality" (Nobel website). Twenty years later, in October 2013, a group of scholars met in Stockholm to commemorate and celebrate Morrison's award, and just as importantly, to critically engage the wealth of scholarship that has sprung up around Morrison's work—both the six novels recognized by the Nobel committee and those works of fiction and criticism published in the two decades afterwards.

The papers delivered at this symposium revealed certainly the ongoing "poetic import" of Morrison's work, yet what they illustrated most compellingly was that there is no one "essential aspect of American reality" to which Morrison's words give voice. Her novels engage contexts and questions ranging from the nature of servitude in the colonial period to the poetics and politics of Harlem in the Jazz Age, from explorations of the class differences that cut across relations between African American individuals and communities to the physical and psychological violence that constituted segregation and Jim Crow. Indeed, it is difficult to identify an "American reality" into which Morrison has not made an exact and searing intervention; even as her novels focus intimately on the lives of African Americans, white Americans are interpellated equally by the ways in which her explorations reveal the operations of whiteness—the disavowals of equality and the miscarriages of justice that went into its creation and maintenance. Moreover, as the international perspective of many of the participants in the symposium demonstrated, Morrison's account of the history of "race" is not even limited to American realities.

At the heart of Morrison's project lies the conviction that acts of language constitute lived realities and thus that language can shape and change these realities as a force of both healing and harm. The lecture she gave on accepting the Nobel Prize takes language as its subject in order to offer a compelling indictment of "dead" language that disables and censors, maintains an unjust *status quo* and, worse, the vampiric languages of sexism, racism, and "theism" that exploit vulnerability and foster division. Such language euphemizes state-sanctioned violence, silences dissent, and rationalizes dominion of one group over another. Evoking the polyphony of language that came about as a result of the collapse of the Tower of Babel, she goes on to celebrate the limitless reaching of language towards the ineffable—language constantly expands the boundaries of what is possible and imaginable. But in the same vein, language can never fully encapsulate the collective trauma of slavery or genocide, nor can it ever totalize individual experiences of violence or loss and it should not aspire to. Yet the striving after such expression can bring about the confrontation with the ineffable necessary for our own comprehension of the nature of trauma. Language, then, for Morrison must be dynamic, must evolve. Narrative, she declaims, must radically bring new subjectivities into being, even in the very moment of its own creation. In short, language must *live*.

Taking Morrison's Nobel lecture as a point of departure, Andrea Sillis' essay, "Forms of Time and Typologies of Culture in the Work of Toni Morrison," argues that Morrison's conceptualization of language itself, and her ideas about the politics of identity formation, are organized by means of a complex network of temporal oppositions. Through close analysis of Morrison's "Nobel Lecture," Sillis demonstrates that language is a medium that is naturally oriented towards the future through both its epistemological function and the creativity of the linguistic imagination. Moreover, this connection between language and the future is inherently politicized since Morrison clearly identifies the open-ended temporality of creative language with freedom of expression. Conversely, she correlates any form of censorship, dogma or political oppression with the temporality of closure, stasis and stagnation, and explicitly locates racism within the retrograde temporal framework she associates with oppressive forms of language.

Moving outwards from the lecture, Sillis goes on to propose that Morrison resists the idea that white America's historical involvement in slavery was a temporary ethical aberration. She suggests rather that its will to dominance stems from a presumption of cultural supremacy that is firmly rooted in Western models of epistemology. This negative assessment is diametrically opposed to Morrison's valorization of the epistemological foundations of black language and culture, which is clearly identified with an interlocative model of African American language and aesthetics, informed, in turn, by their origins in oral traditions. Morrison expressly describes this model as incorporating folk-cultural attitudes towards knowledge and identity, which naturally accommodate ambiguity and tolerate difference. In view of this celebration of the linguistic dynamism of orality, Sillis proposes that Morrison draws on insights provided by the implicit temporal ordering of her philosophy of language to pinpoint the critical sources of disparities between "black" and "white" language practices, and their associated perceptions of identity. For Morrison, African American discourse "lives" because of its ability to adapt and accommodate difference.

Chapter two turns to French-language versions of Morrison's first novel to illustrate the ways in which her language lives on in translation. In "Toni Morrison's *The Bluest Eye*: Lost and Found in Translation" Lynn Penrod considers a critical question that is often overlooked by literary scholars: the fate of a particular text, or indeed, of a particular author's entire body of work, when it is translated. Nobel Prize laureates in literature have long provided lively debates worldwide on this issue. The market in literary translation is dominated by English speakers and readers desperately seeking translations of texts originally published in unfamiliar languages. Literary translators work feverishly to meet publishers' deadlines, and while some readers and reviewers may be left pondering the accuracy of their work, demand has been met and most readers are satisfied. Yet we seldom worry about the fate of an English-language Nobel Prize winner whose works will be translated or re-translated into untold numbers of languages once the award is announced. Penrod asks, therefore: So what do we mean when we speak of "Toni Morrison in translation?" What actually happens to the work of any author as it crosses not only linguistic borders but entire cultural frontiers as well? How do the theory and practice of "translating" Toni Morrison's novels affect Morrison criticism, analysis, reputation, or pedagogy? Penrod takes as her case study for thinking through these questions the French version of Morrison's first novel, *The Bluest Eye*, translated as *L'oeil le plus bleu* by Jean Guiloineau and published in Paris by Christian Bourgois Editeur in 1994. Using Roman Jakobson's well-known three levels of translational competence—intralingual, interlingual, and intersemiotic—Penrod analyzes the particular challenges this novel poses to the literary translator concluding that the accurate translation of Morrison's novel requires a variation on Jakobson's intersemiotic level: a competence that she terms inter- or trans-cultural competence.

Chapter three demonstrates the remarkable adaptability of Morrison's literary imagination. "Teaching Toni Morrison to a Culturally Diverse

Class" recounts Sangita Rayamajhi's experiences of teaching western and non-western fiction at The Asian University for Women in Bangladesh. This university is a place where the histories and experiences of collective memory and social, structural, and political inequality are constantly being redefined. The multiculturalism of the classroom is nevertheless marked by different histories of religious dogmatism, and it is into this setting that Rayamajhi introduces Morrison through her first novel, *The Bluest Eye*. Despite her fears that students would find this historically and culturally laden text inaccessible, her students were not only able to understand the text's subtlety and nuance but were able to transfer the issues it explores out of their western context and into an Asian one. Students recognized and understood Morrison's depiction of discrimination, isolation, hierarchy, race, and class in relation to women's bodies under patriarchy and were able to make sense of the multiple structures of inequality she represents, relating them to issues of caste, class, untouchability, patriarchy, women, and to the stratification in the cultures of South Asia, South East Asia and East Asia.

Bodies are, of course, central to Morrison's work from Pecola Breedlove's neglected and abused body, to Sethe's "chokecherry" tree of scars, to Florens' feet that are finally conditioned to be tough like cedar. She writes of the body in visceral ways that remind us—as the young women of the Asian University show us—of our own somatic fragility. In "Bodies, Music, and Embodied Cognition in Toni Morrison's Fictional Works" Anna Iatsenko illustrates the ways in which Morrison uses the body to tell stories that transcend fictional ontology to communicate meaning on a number of levels. In some works, the bodies of characters act as traces of the history of slavery by quite literally revealing the inscriptions of its trauma. In others, bodies oscillate between the transcendent and the immanent to reveal the mechanisms of embodied memory. Indeed, the intricacy with which Morrison works on and with bodies reveals the complexity of corporeality and the centrality of the body to our perception of and interaction with the world. Iatsenko engages Morrison's use of the body in order to discuss perception from a phenomenological point of view. As Maurice Merlau-Ponty's work has suggested, the body is the primary vehicle of interaction with and understanding of the world. This postulate, which works against Cartesian logic, has more recently been confirmed by a number of neuro-scientific studies that have been able to map out the neurological pathways of cognition. However, as Iatsenko argues, Morrison's work provides a space where the text embodies both voices and music, complicating

8

Merleau-Ponty's paradigm of embodied cognition by introducing the importance of the domain of sound perception. Morrison's use of music, song and voice, deeply rooted in African-American traditional aesthetic forms, exceeds the mere presence of musical references in her novels. Indeed, through the use of music in her fiction, Morrison points to the fact that mechanisms of embodied consciousness are also deeply connected to music as is revealed by the interplay between form and content in her work. Language lives through its relationship to the body—the way it is heard and the way it is felt.

Voice and embodiment are equally central to chapter five, "African American Maternal Experience in Toni Morrison's *Beloved*." In this essay, Giulia Grillo Mikrut discusses the representation of the African American female body in Morrison's Pulitzer Prize-winning novel to show how this representation tracks the process of self-actualization of the female characters. Self-actualisation is here defined as the process by which the female characters achieve a fully realized subjectivity and obtain an audible voice in the societies in which they live. In *Beloved*, it is the initially fragmented body that ultimately expresses the coherent development of the female mind, spirit, and voice. This chapter considers the patterns and devices chosen by Morrison to show the African American female body as a key factor in the depiction of African American women's subjectivity. At the beginning of the novel, women's bodies are "fragmented" in the same way that their voices are disjointed and fractured. For different reasons and in order to survive, these characters must move on from this fragmentation by embarking on a journey towards self-actualisation. Grillo Mikrut analyzes how Morrison employs the motif of the development of the maternal body and female voice with the aim of illustrating these women's eventual claim to agency in society. Voice and body are inseparable in achieving fully realized subjectivity. Demonstrating that black women's voices and bodies are inaudible and invisible at the beginning of the novel, this chapter shows how female characters move from marginalization and fragmentation to centrality and wholeness, eventually reaching self-actualization.

Black women's bodies have often been overdetermined by their relationship to maternity. As powerless slave mothers in the nineteenth century and as outraged victims of ongoing violence against their outlawed male children in the twenty-first, the African-American mother is a figure of trauma. Yet Morrison's imagination of this figure does not less us categorize her so reductively. Hence, in chapter six, "The Black Mother as Murderess: William Faulkner's *Requiem for a Nun* and Toni Morrison's *Beloved*," Lucy

Buzacott considers the characters of Nancy Mannigoe in William Faulkner's 1950 novel *Requiem for a Nun* and Sethe in Toni Morrison's 1987 novel *Beloved* as versions of the black mother as murderess. Buzacott explores how both Nancy and Sethe complicate received versions of black maternity through an act of violent maternal potency. Both Nancy and Sethe ultimately kill a child in their care, but while Sethe murders her own child, Nancy is a mammy, a maternal surrogate, and the child she kills is not her own but the infant child of her white employee. While both murders speak to the maternal suffering of black women during and after slavery, what changes when the murdering mother is not a mother, but a mammy and the child is not black but white? Buzacott examines how Nancy Mannigoe acts as both mammy and monster within the text of *Requiem* and explores the ways in which her representation differs from Morrison's Sethe and how both figures speak to the problems of race, gender, sexuality, and maternity in the post-War American South. In a dynamic reversal of literary historical chronology, Buzacott's reading of *Beloved* reanimates and revises our understanding of Faulkner's much earlier text.

Once again taking up the representation of outranged maternity in Morrison's work chapter seven, "A Valediction Forbidding Mo'nin: Melancholic Community in Toni Morrison's *Beloved*," looks beyond the maternal melodrama that dominates scholarship on Beloved and explores the hitherto under-analyzed relationship between sisters Beloved and Denver. As Hilary Emmett notes, in the closing pages of the novel, Paul D asks Denver, "You think she sure 'nough your sister?" Denver replies, "At times. At times I think she was—more" (266). Emmett argues that Denver's understanding of Beloved as her sister, and as signifying something "more" is revealing in that it raises the question of what sisterhood might have meant in the immediate aftermath of slavery's abolition. It gestures to sisterhood's excess, its unconfineable significance in United States' history. The something "more" that Beloved embodies is commonly understood as the uncontainability of the traumatic memory of slavery, the eternally recurring "rememory" which cannot be kept at bay, and as such, inhibits the free and forward movement of the community of former slaves. This chapter extends this idea of excess into an account of the limits of sisterhood in American political life both during the period of Reconstruction in which the novel is set, and also, speculatively, into the 1980s when the novel was written. As Morrison herself has emphasized, *Beloved* was written with the intention of revealing what lay behind what Lydia Maria Child termed the "veil" drawn over the most "monstrous features" of slavery. Despite

Child's rhetoric, the alliance forged between "conscientious and reflecting [white] women at the North" and their "sisters in bondage" was predicated on the slave narrator's elision of details that might prove too indelicate for white women's ears. The rhetoric of sisterhood was deployed by abolitionist movements in both Britain and America, presumably in order both to insist upon the common humanity of slaves, and to harness the momentum of the abolitionist cause to movements calling for women's rights—an alliance that would cause no little consternation among advocates of the cause of women's suffrage. Emmett shows that a political community based on an ideal of sisterhood is necessarily predicated on the expulsion of the traumatized and traumatizing sister, and is undeniably melancholic.

Tuire Valkeakari turns similarly to the uneasy alliances between black and white women in chapter eight, "After Eden: Constructs of Home, House, and Racial Difference in Toni Morrison's *A Mercy*." *A Mercy*, Valkeakari writes, can be viewed through the related lenses of movement, migration, dislocation, and journeying. Morrison has written about "home" throughout her career—that is, about domiciles and families, as well as about places of belonging in a more abstract and geopolitical sense. While scholars have previously placed Morrison's aptly titled 1997 essay "Home" in dialogue with *Paradise*, this chapter argues that her reflections in "Home" are extremely relevant to *A Mercy*, too: such pivotal themes and motifs of Morrison's essay as the trope of Eden, constructs of home (what she in "Home" calls "a radical distinction between the metaphor of house and the metaphor of home") and early colonial American racial formations all play significant roles in her ninth novel, whose present action is set in 1690. Morrison embeds the trope of Eden in *A Mercy* by casting the Anglo-Dutch settler Jacob Vaark as an "American Adam" and by asking, in the process, who has the right to belong in America and call it "home." Where Leo Marx famously put "the machine in the garden [of Eden/America]," Morrison, in turn, puts race—in addition to social class—in the garden. Thus, she places the trope of the American Adam in dialogue with race, racialization, and racism and, in so doing, urges us to examine the role that racial formations played in American social relations even prior to the United States' nationhood. This novel, published in 2008 in the lead-up to the election of Barack Obama as the first African American president of the United States thus looks backward in order to engage the present, and tentatively imagine a future. For Morrison, the myth of "racial" difference, and therefore racial hierarchy can only be dismantled by a return to a time before which this social construct exerted a stranglehold on communal life.

Aoi Mori links Morrison's representation of a "pre-racial" America in *A Mercy* explicitly to contemporary concerns regarding race by reading the novel alongside Morrison's earlier critical analysis of race in America, *Race Matters*. Barack Obama's political success signifies to some that we live in a "post-racial" era, an age in which race is no longer a barrier to material success and social significance. Yet, for Morrison, the twinned specters of race and racism continue to haunt American society. Morrison described *A Mercy* as an attempt to "remove race from slavery." Mori's chapter explores how the concept of race is constructed in Vaark's household and then in American society by examining the historical background embedded in *A Mercy* and referring to some of Morrison's other works, such as *The Bluest Eye*, "Home," *Playing in the Dark*, and *Desdemona*, which also scrutinize race issues. Finally, Mori points to the skillful strategy used by Morrison to deconstruct racial hierarchies and thereby recover the narratives of those relegated to the periphery of society.

Home and nationhood are again twinned concerns in Morrison's most recent novel, *Home*. In "This house is strange": Digging for American Memory of Trauma, or Healing the "Social" in Toni Morrison's "*Home*," Laura Castor reveals the way this novel asks us to question the social, political, and personal illusions of "America." The notion of America as a "home" free from the weight of history and fertile ground for numerous opportunities for self-invention is revealed to be illusory. As readers have come to expect from Morrison, the seemingly simple notion of 'home' has multiple meanings, both cultural and personal. Morrison's shifting narrative perspectives on the stories of Cee and Frank lay bare even the most hidden violence of Jim Crow, but also open spaces for agency and healing—healing that honors, rather than seeks to erase scars. More broadly, her narrators' representations of 'home' and 'homelessness' provide a fulcrum for the reader to question American collective memory. Ideas of home may be narrated differently through prisms of age, geography, and historical moment, as well as economies of race, class, and gender inequality. Castor's analysis of this novel asks: at what cost, and for the sake of what expanded notions of truth, must her characters mourn their pasts? In asking and answering this question through her novel, Castor proposes that Morrison provokes her readers to take more seriously their own journeys toward greater social awareness.

The essays in this collection implicitly and explicitly take up Morrison's clarion call to vivify language. They approach Morrison's imagined worlds and non-fiction writings from a variety of disciplinary perspectives, from

the straight forwardly literary-critical, to the phenomenological and peda-
gogical. They engage her words by elaborating on their meaning, offering
readings of her literary texts that highlight their intertextuality, their
proliferating conversations with other texts and contexts, and even other
languages. In some, Morrison's words give life to authors no longer with us,
in others we are encouraged to resituate her writing in unfamiliar contexts
in order to highlight the multiplicity of meanings generated by her work.
The essays offer rich testimony to the life-giving properties of Morrison's
language and seek to contribute to the ongoing afterlife of her work by
adding to the scholarly conversations and debates animated by her
extraordinary literary career.

Kerstin W. Shands and Giulia Grillo Mikrut
Stockholm, May, 2014

Forms of Time and Typologies of Culture: Language, Time, and Identity in the Work of Toni Morrison

Andrea Sillis

This essay examines the connection between the themes of language, time, and identity in the work of Toni Morrison. It considers, in particular, the central role played by time in her critical analyses of the contested fields of race and identity, in what she has described as "the wholly racialized society that is the United States" (*Playing* xii).

The title of the essay consciously echoes that of Bakhtin's: "Forms of Time and the Chronotope in the Novel: Notes toward a Historical Poetics" (*Dialogic* 84-258). His radically temporalized conceptualization of linguistic consciousness is encapsulated in the statements that "every entry into the sphere of meaning is accomplished only through the gates of the chronotope;" and that "in the literary artistic chronotope, spatial and temporal indicators are fused into one carefully thought-out, concrete whole. Time, as it were, thickens, takes on flesh, becomes artistically visible" (*Dialogic* 258; 84). His idea that the "chronotope in literature has an intrinsic *generic* significance" (84-5, emphasis in original), together with his definition of "utterances and their types, that is, speech genres" as "the drive belts from the history of society to the history of language" (*Speech Genres* 65), is particularly interesting in the context of Morrison's generic (rather than genetic) definitions of black identity. Their work is also directly comparable on account of pronounced similarities in the temporal organization of their typological analyses of cultural forms.

The essay does not, however, present a Bakhtinian analysis of Morrison's work. It argues that her perception of the underlying temporality of linguistic and cultural forms represents an organic component of her own cultural, generic, and intellectual perspective. The large body of work which she has produced as both a highly acclaimed novelist and a respected literary and cultural critic is entirely permeated by a thoroughly temporalized lexicon. Close analysis of this thematic preoccupation reveals that she routinely configures the coincidence between the categories of language, time, and identity in such a way that her ideas about language itself, and the politics of identity formation, are organized by means of a complex arrangement of temporal oppositions. This would seem to indicate that the category of time lies at the very center of her thinking about linguistic and cultural forms, and that she perceives a deep structural connection between temporality and linguistic consciousness itself.

In addition, her skill as a historical novelist is enhanced by a theoretical interest in diverse modes of historical perception, and in the role played by historical discourse in conditioning perceptions of identity. Indeed, the acuity of her handling of historical time has been recognized in studies by Paul Gilroy and Homi Bhabha, both of which have a particular focus, black or subaltern identity and temporality. Gilroy, in *The Black Atlantic*, cites her work as exemplary of "black writers whose minority modernism can be defined precisely through its imaginative proximity to forms of terror that surpass understanding and lead back from contemporary racial violence, through lynching, towards the temporal and ontological rupture of the middle passage" (222). Bhabha analyzed Morrison's representation of historical experience in *Beloved* extensively in *The Location of Culture*, and acknowledged that her work had been "formative in [his] thinking on narrative and historical temporality" (ix).

This essay suggests, therefore, that the coherence of Morrison's work as a whole rests on the foundation of a tightly argued and internally consistent philosophy of language, which coheres around a highly systematic conceptualization of time. It hopes to demonstrate that this radically temporalized philosophy of language exerts systemic effects on Morrison's work as a whole, fundamentally conditioning the conceptual parameters of her wider engagements with the politics of writing and representation, and significantly facilitating her critical investigations into the relationship of dominance and subordination within which black and white identity politics in America have historically been established and defined.

Morrison's "Nobel Lecture" provides the main source of textual evidence used here in support of these ideas. Several factors combine to make this text exemplify the thesis that her invocations of temporality are symptomatic of a systemic theoretical perspective on language and identity, which

16

is grounded on her sense of the implicit temporal ordering of cultural and linguistic forms.

First of all, this lecture presents what is probably Morrison's most sustained treatment of her conceptualization of language. In addition, the text is permeated by a dense metaphorical network of conjoined linguistic and temporal associations, so that although time is not her overt focus here, its pervasive sub-textual presence nonetheless exerts a significant influence over the conceptual and structural organization of the piece as a whole. I would argue, in fact, that the level of fusion between temporal and linguistic signifiers she presents here is such that facts about language can also be read as facts about time. The imprint of time therefore appears as a palimpsest showing through her entire discourse about language.

The Lecture also offers clear evidence in support of the idea that Morrison perceives a deep structural connection not only between forms of temporal and linguistic consciousness, but also between the temporality of linguistic forms and identity formation. More precisely, given that the content of the Lecture is set firmly in the context of post-slavery America, it clearly incorporates references to the temporal and linguistic modelling that she adopts to articulate her insights into the radically divergent cultural forms which underpin the construction and ascription of racialized identity in the USA.

And finally, this functions as something of a hybrid text, occupying a liminal position between critical and creative writing. Consequently, it allows us to trace the systemic effects of Morrison's philosophy of language as she formulates what is simultaneously a creative and critical response to the task she has described as "trying to come to some terms about 'race' and writing" ("Unspeakable" 3).

The Nobel Lecture in Literature

Morrison makes language itself the central theme of her "Nobel Lecture," and draws together in this short but complex composition all the main elements which combine to condition her concept of language. However, this statement about her personal and professional relationship with language contains no programmatic or direct statements about her identity politics, theoretical perspective or philosophical position. Instead, she presents a story, opening her Lecture with a traditional tale in which a group of children approach a blind old woman and ask her to tell them whether the bird they have in their hands is alive or dead.

Morrison states that she chooses to read the bird as language, and as she imagines the exchange between the old woman and the children, which develops out of the scenario presented in the oral tale, this Lecture quickly becomes a genuine act of oral narration in its own right. Consequently, oral narrative itself, as opposed to the print-based discipline of philosophical discourse, becomes the medium through which she chooses to articulate her philosophy of language.[1]

Moreover, this is not just a stylistic choice: by adopting this narrative framework, Morrison immediately dissociates her account of language not just from the disciplinary conventions of Anglo-American philosophy, but also from the abstract theoretical framework within which it has traditionally been articulated. This categorical distinction is also signaled by the content of the oral tale, which functions to constrain the conceptual parameters of the theory of language it presents in accordance with the conditions of its specific setting.

For instance, within the context of the oral tale, the blind, old woman would only know that the bird was alive if she heard it singing, and so the metaphor of the bird for language equates living language with song. This establishes that Morrison's definition of language is derived from its performative aspect as speech, rather than from its formal aspect as a set of semantic units and syntactic rules. It therefore places her concept of language within the personalized and historicized parameters of the utterance, rather than the explicitly depersonalized and a-temporal parameters of philosophical abstraction.

The metaphor of the bird for language is therefore central to Morrison's exposition of her conceptualization of language insofar as it encapsulates the temporal, linguistic, and cultural dualisms which are at the structural center of this piece. Whilst the image of a bird is commonly made to stand for the concept of language in a general sense, by placing this bird in the hands of these children, Morrison encourages her audience to visualize it as an actually existent bird with a concrete, corporeal identity of its own, rather than as the notional or disembodied idea of a bird.

---

[1] This brings to mind Barbara Christian's comment that "people of color have always theorized—but in forms quite different from the Western form of abstract logic. And I am inclined to say that our theorizing (and I intentionally use the verb rather than the noun) is often in narrative forms, in the stories we create, in riddles and proverbs, in the play with language, since dynamic rather than fixed ideas seem more to our liking" (349).

The challenge which the children issue to the old woman to tell them whether the bird is alive or dead then takes the idea of physical embodiment a little further, since the possibility of mortality which is introduced in that question immediately imports an undeniably existential element into the concept of language for which the bird stands. Morrison emphasizes the significance of the existential aspect of her metaphor still further when she says that "the question the children put to [the woman] – Is [the bird] living or dead? – is not unreal because she thinks of language as susceptible to death, erasure, certainly imperiled and salvageable only by an effort of the will" ("Nobel" 200).[2]

The idea that language itself may be susceptible to death enacts a radical personification of the theory of language so conceived. The existential metaphor forces us to conceptualize language as physically incarnated in subjects who must be materially embodied in spatio-temporally specific historical contexts. This is a theoretical approach, therefore, which programmatically conflates the categories of language and identity, whilst also simultaneously imbuing its concept of language with a very specific form of temporal sensibility. Being fundamentally subject-centered, it invokes not the abstract temporality of infinite chronological time, but a humanized version of time which is bounded by consciousness of death and regulated by memory rather than the clock; a form of time, in fact, which is intimately bound up with the consciousness of personal identity.

The existential dualism which is inherent in the opposition between life and death goes on to structure the metaphorical organization of the conceptual content of the entire Lecture, thereby playing an important role in facilitating the articulation of the distinctive philosophy of language which animates Morrison's work as a whole. In addition, this trope allows her to present living and dead language as two distinct forms of linguistic consciousness, each with their own temporal signature, and each embodying an entire cultural and philosophical perspective, or episteme, in its own right. Ultimately, therefore, the temporal opposition which is central to the metaphor of the living-or-dead bird serves to underpin the typological analysis of cultural forms which emerges as the Lecture progresses.

Morrison consistently characterizes living language as being naturally oriented towards the future, and this temporal signature is woven into all the statements about living language which run through the Lecture. For

---

[2] All further references in this section are to the "Nobel Lecture," unless identified otherwise.

example, she describes language as having "nuanced, complex, midwifery properties" (201), and says that "word-work is sublime [...] because it is generative" (203). She identifies this orientation of language to the future with the potential creativity of the linguistic imagination and the multiple possible interpretations and perspectives it can open up, stating that "the vitality of language lies in its ability to limn the actual, imagined, and possible lives of its speakers, readers, writers. [...] It arcs toward the place where meaning may lie" (202-03).[3] Her acute sense of the openness of language to the future stems also from her appreciation of its epistemological function: she sees language as a medium through which knowledge can be both found and made, and insists that "unmolested language surges toward knowledge" (203).

Morrison's focus on language as a living thing produces an effusion of positive and productive associations. However, this link between language and the future is inherently politicized, since she clearly associates the creativity of the linguistic consciousness not only with the future but also with freedom of thought and expression. This brings into play the flip side of the existential paradigm, which equates dead language with the politics of censorship and oppression. She is acutely aware that language is also the medium through which subjection and domination takes place, and writes extensively here about the danger presented to living language by dominant and domineering cultures, noting that "oppressive language does more than represent violence; it is violence" (201). Moreover, access to the evolutionary, epistemological potential of language is forcibly barred by oppressive language, which "does more than represent the limits of knowledge; it limits knowledge. [...] Sexist language, racist language, theistic language–all are typical of the policing languages of mastery, and cannot, do not permit new knowledge or encourage the mutual exchange of ideas" (201).

The suppression of living language always entails both violence against an oppressed Other and an element of temporal deformation in Morrison's work. She describes dominant cultures as explicitly attempting to universalize their own cultural values and eternalize their own position of dominance. By aggressively suppressing alternative worldviews and dissonant voices, they reduce diversity to a contrived form of consensus and ideological uniformity.

---

[3] This sense that language is oriented towards the future is found throughout her work. She notes, for example, that 'the imagination that produces work which bears and invites rereadings, which motions to future readings as well as contemporary ones, implies a shareable world and an endlessly flexible language" (Playing xii).

This brings into play a temporal perspective organized around notions of permanence, closure and fixity. Throughout her writing on the subject of cultural dominance, she invariably correlates political oppression with corrupted forms of temporal consciousness, describing it in terms of paralysis, stasis, stagnation, and death. She states here, for example, that "a dead language is not only one no longer spoken or written, it is unyielding language content to admire its own paralysis." She also describes it as "calcified," "disabled and disabling," and "mov[ing] relentlessly to the bottom line and the bottomed-out mind" (200).

A deeply sinister form of agency accompanies the sense of temporal paralysis in Morrison's account of dead language. She states that "however moribund, it is not without effect for it actively thwarts the intellect, stalls conscience, suppresses human potential" (200). Her descriptions of dead language consciously draw on gothic images of the living dead and vampirism to suggest that it actually feeds off the identities of others.[4] For example, she says that "the heart of such language is languishing, or perhaps not beating at all" (202), and describes it as being not only "dumb," but "predatory" (200), "language that drinks blood, laps vulnerabilities" (201). The sense of temporal deformation, which constantly accompanies her accounts of cultural dominance is clearly intensified in the existential paradox contained in the idea of the living dead.

These inhuman images of the living dead also register Morrison's sense of revulsion at the inhumane politics and ethics of dominant language. We are told that dead language "leaves [...] no access to human instincts" (201). It does not recognize the humanity of others, and in perceiving other human subjects as radically Other, it enacts a process of objectification which is explicitly dehumanizing. Reification enacts an ontological re-description of the Other, allowing it to be cast as sub-human. This places the Other-as-object beyond the reach of any system of ethics normally governing interactions between human subjects, and consequently sanctions behavior which would otherwise be considered inhumane.

Morrison sees the objectification of the Other not just as an ethical evasion which normalizes abuse, however, but as an identity manoeuvre with reflexive effects. In reifying and dehumanizing the Other, the dominant subject invokes a radical disjunction between self and Other, and so

---

[4] See Rice, Chapter 5, "'Who's Eating Whom?': The Discourse of Cannibalism in Narratives of the Black and White Atlantic," for a discussion of images of cannibalism in historical and literary discourse about race.

risks falling into a pathological state of solipsism.[5] She describes dominant language, for instance, as having "no desire or purpose other than maintaining the free range of its own narcotic narcissism" (200), and clearly regards dominant language not just as dehumanizing but as dehumanized.[6]

Morrison sums up her sense that dogmatic language is itself dehumanized in her description of official language, "smitheryed to sanction ignorance and preserve privilege," as "a suit of armor polished to shocking glitter, a husk from which the knight departed long ago" (200). The suit of armor is simultaneously a cliché of power; an empty, inanimate, and abstract simulacrum of the living human subject; and an invocation of temporal stasis. The metaphor also emphasizes the reflective surface of the armor, bringing to mind, once again, the pool into which the original Narcissus gazed in a state of suicidal self-obsession.

In this sense, cultural dominance is characterized not only by a loss of the temporal dynamic associated with language conceived as an open dialogue with alterity, but also by a concomitant vitiation of the processes at the heart of identity formation. In the context of this debate on the politics of identity formation, it is significant that Morrison describes "word-work" as "sublime" not just "because it is generative," but also because it "makes meaning that secures our difference, our human difference—the way in which we are like no other life" (203).

This statement encapsulates the idea that Morrison's concept of living language, as well as occupying a completely different temporal register to that of dead language, is also associated with an entirely different ethical sensibility. In radically personalizing her concept of living language, therefore, she presents it not just as essentially human, but as fundamentally humane.

Indeed, a sense of ethical awareness is integral to the concept of living language as depicted in the "Nobel Lecture." The old woman in the story describes language as both "a living thing" and as "agency, an act with consequences" (200). The emphasis on agency incorporates both a sense of responsibility for others and a benevolent attitude towards alterity. For example, living language is described here as having "life-sustaining pro-

---

[5] Morrison has noted elsewhere that "the trauma of racism is, for the racist and the victim, the severe fragmentation of the self, and has always seemed to me a cause (not a symptom) of psychosis—strangely of no interest to psychiatry" ("Unspeakable" 16).

[6] This idea is reflected in her statement that "slavery broke the world in half, it broke it in every way. It broke Europe. It made them into something else, it made them slave masters, it made them crazy. [...] They had to dehumanize, not just the slaves but themselves" (Gilroy, *Small Acts* 178).

perties" (203), and as being "a device for grappling with meaning, providing guidance or expressing love" (200).

Whereas dead language subverts the normal flow of biological cycles of time, living language nurtures the young and passes tradition and experience on through successive generations. It is described, in the words of the children in the story, as "song, [...] literature, [a] poem full of vitamins, [...] history connected to experience that you can pass along to help us start strong" (205). The life-sustaining properties of living language are situated within the context of a caring, intergenerational community, as is clearly indicated in the children's request for a transfer of historical and generic knowledge. This represents a healthy consciousness of past, present, and future as mediated through cycles of biological progression and the transmission of cultural and historical memory.

Although this Lecture begins by condemning all forms of oppression, its actual setting in racialized America means that its attention comes to rest inevitably on the devastating effects of racism on American society as a whole. Morrison explicitly identifies racism, both here and throughout her work as a whole, with oppressive forms of language. She has developed a temporally inflected conceptualization of the link between language and power, which she uses to characterize the relationship between America's dominant white, and subordinated black cultures.

The temporal deformation ascribed here to racist language is not just a notional or theoretical invocation of time, but reflects her claim that the way in which the dominant white culture relates to its own historical past and potential future has been seriously compromised by its own ideology of racial supremacy. She has stated, for instance, that

> we live in a land where the past is always erased and America is the innocent future in which immigrants can come and start over, where the slate is clean. The past is absent or it's romanticized. This culture doesn't encourage dwelling on, let alone coming to terms with, the truth about the past. (Gilroy, Small Acts 179)

Similarly, she has asked whether America is "a country so hungry for a purely imagined past of innocence and clarity that it is willing to subvert the future and, in fact, to declare that there is none, in order to wallow in illusion?" ("Writers Together" 397).[7]

---

[7] See Morrison's Jefferson Lecture in the Humanities, "The Future of Time," for an extended treatment of the ethical and temporal deformations invoked by Western

Within the "Nobel Lecture," Morrison graphically depicts dominant political language spilling out into the community as a whole and leaving a trail of death and destruction. For example, the old woman thinks that: "there is and will be rousing language to keep citizens armed and arming; slaughtered and slaughtering in the malls, courthouses, post offices, playgrounds, bedrooms and boulevards; stirring, memorializing language to mask the pity and waste of needless death" (201). This presents an extraordinary picture of a fundamentally pathologized society, which has been totally dehumanized by the violence inherent in its own founding mythologies of national identity.

The old woman also states that "in her country" (that is to say, in America) "children have bitten their tongues off and use bullets instead to iterate the voice of speechlessness" (200). Once again, Morrison associates silenced speech with violence, and since bullets represent both death and language here, this image immediately invokes the temporal dead-end of dominant ideology.[8] The image is doubly disturbing because the children are depicted as both victims and instruments of dominant language. This would seem to signify not only that patterns of cultural dominance are passed on through generations, but that this society, in corrupting its own children in this manner, is sabotaging its own future.

In presenting white America as a dominant culture here, Morrison seems to go further than ascribing its historical involvement in slavery to a temporary ethical aberration. She tracks the chain of associations between dominant language, oppression, and corrupted time right back to its source in the ideological and epistemological foundations of modern Western discourse. For example, she finds evidence of oppressive language not only in the "mindless media" but also in the "language [...] of politics and history," the "calcified language of the academy," "the commodity driven language of science," and "the malign language of law-without-ethics" (201-02).

This amounts to a comprehensive attack on the authoritative discourses of Western rationalism, which have traditionally functioned to legitimate knowledge and underpin judgments of cultural value. Morrison seems to be suggesting here that the ideology of racial superiority is firmly embedded in

---

apocalyptic perceptions of history. See also Christians⬚ especially Chapter Three, "Morrison's Modernist Apocalyptics," for a discussion of these themes.

[8] This is reminiscent of her description of racism as "a death-dealing ideology" in "Home" (5).

the very roots of Western models of epistemology.[9] This is consistent with her description of white cultural supremacy in the West as "whiteness as ideology" in her Tanner Lecture on Human Values, "Unspeakable Things Unspoken" (16).

In that Lecture, Morrison argued that the academic establishment performs an aggressively conservative political function in legislating cultural value against the benchmark of its own canonical texts. The temporal perspective embodied in the conservative canon is specifically organized around the task of perpetuating control over perceptions of cultural value. She makes this argument very forcefully in the following comment:

> Canon building is Empire building. Canon defense is national defense. Canon debate, whatever the terrain, nature and range (of criticism, of history, of the history of knowledge, of the definition of language, the universality of aesthetic principles, the sociology of art, the humanistic imagination), is the clash of cultures. And *all* of the interests are vested. ("Unspeakable" 8, emphasis in original)

In the "Nobel Lecture," Morrison clearly associates dogmatic, or dead, language with the epistemological foundations of Western rationalism when she describes it as "arrogant pseudo-empirical language crafted to lock creative people into cages of inferiority and hopelessness" (202). Conversely, she explicitly associates living language here with an entirely different epistemological paradigm. In direct contrast to the rationalist desire to classify phenomena, codify knowledge, and discover universal laws (which are, by definition, immutable), the old woman in the story suggests that "the force" and "felicity" of language lies "in its reach towards the *ineffable*" (203, emphasis added).

The old woman herself actually personifies a traditional, non-Western, epistemological perspective. At the very beginning of the Lecture, she is identified as a griot or guru, and her intelligence is described as "rural," or folk "wisdom." The fact that the source of her knowledge lies in "lore" and

---

[9] Edward Said, in his seminal study *Orientalism*, also identified Western hegemony with its conviction of cultural and epistemological supremacy. He defined the "relationship between Occident and Orient" as one "of power, of domination, of varying degrees of a complex hegemony" (5), and stated that what different forms of Orientalism all have in common (and he cites German, Anglo-French and later American forms) is "a kind of intellectual *authority* over the Orient within Western culture" (19, emphasis in original). He describes authority as being "virtually indistinguishable from certain ideas it dignifies as true, and from traditions, perceptions, and judgements it forms, transmits, reproduces" (19-20).

"clairvoyance," means that it is automatically discredited by the dominant culture, represented here as the city, "where the intelligence of rural prophets is the source of much amusement" (198). This invokes a radical disjunction between the epistemological models of modern Western and traditional societies, and also signals a hiatus between their respective modes of historical consciousness.[10] In addition, the ambivalent status of the old woman as "both the law and transgression" among her own people puts her totally outside the either/or logic of rationalism (198).

It is highly significant, moreover, that wherever we find the trace of living language in this Lecture, it is associated with the African American subjects it presents. Within the Lecture, for example, direct speech itself, as opposed to abstract formulations of dead language such as "the voice of speechlessness" (200), is the prerogative of the old woman, the children, and Morrison herself. Morrison identifies herself with the old woman as a black female writer, who represents the cultural, ethical, and epistemological values of African America. This is consistent with her personal identification with an interlocative model of black language and aesthetics, which has been comprehensively generically informed by traditions that originated in its oral cultural practices. [11]

The children in the story, despite the fact that the old woman "does not know their color, gender or homeland" (199), also align themselves with the cultural and epistemological paradigm of Black America, since it transpires that they have come not to intimidate her but to ask for guidance. Although they begin by asking the old woman to "make up a story" (205), they actually proceed to improvise the desired narrative themselves. In so doing, they function as oral narrators in their own right, thereby identifying closely with the old woman and Morrison herself. Furthermore, the content of the children's narrative also links them to the black history. It registers the suffering and loss incurred through the experience of slavery, but also

---

[10] See Bhabha's discussion of Fanon's essay, "The Fact of Blackness," and the disjunction between the temporality of Western modernity and that ascribed to the colonized. (Chapter 12, "'Race,' time and the revision of modernity.") Consider also, in this context, Hegel's comment (taken from a series of lectures originally given between 1821 and 1831) that "Africa [...] is no historical part of the World; it has no movement or development to exhibit. [...] What we properly understand by Africa, is the Unhistorical, Undeveloped Spirit, still involved in the conditions of mere nature" (99).

[11] Morrison has stated, for example: "My métier is Black. [...] I wanted to write literature that was irrevocably, indisputably Black, not because its characters were, or because I was, but because it took as its creative task and sought as its credentials those recognized and verifiable principles of Black art" ("Memory" 388-389).

represents, in the singing and melodies of the slaves, the creativity and vitality of black culture, and the survival of its generic forms.

This fragment of imagined slave narrative also concentrates the opposition between living and dead language, which structures the piece as a whole. Whilst the slaves are associated here with signs of life, such as birth ("placenta in a field" [206]), song, breath, the warmth of bodies and the sun, they are actually moving into the domain of the dead language of racism, which is signified here by the freezing cold.

The slaves are being transported in a wagon into slavery from ships at the shoreline, and at a stop on the road they are brought food and drink by a boy and girl at an inn. We are told that at this stop they are also offered "something more" by the girl: "a glance into the eyes of the ones she serves [...] a look. They look back" (207). This look signifies both human contact and mutual recognition between human subjects. By the time they reach the next stop, however, the slaves will have entered the jurisdiction of a slave economy within which they will be fully objectified and dehumanized. This categorical change of status is signified through the temporal closure contained in the statement that "the next stop will be their last" (207).

The interaction between the old woman and the children is also highly significant in terms of the exposition it presents of the concept of living language. The dynamic of this oral tale actually hinges on language conceived as dialogue between interlocutors. The potential for dialogue seems to break down at two points: when the old woman thinks that the children are using language as an "instrument through which power is exercised" (199); and when the children perceive the old woman's cryptic answer as signifying a refusal to engage, or a "retreat into the singularity of isolation, in sophisticated, privileged space" (204). At these points, textual references to power, arrogance, and isolation infiltrate the text to indicate the presence of dead language, which takes the form, here, of a perceived failure to communicate subject to subject. As soon as the old woman's silence provokes the children into speech, however, a real dialogue can be started, and it transpires that this provocation of genuine dialogue was the old woman's objective all along. The Lecture closes with the following statement from the old woman: "I trust you with the bird that is not in your hands because you have truly caught it. Look. How lovely it is, this thing we have done—together" (207).

It seems clear that, in basing her "Nobel Lecture" on this exchange, Morrison simultaneously contrives to dramatize the principle of living language as dialogue, and to identify living language with the antiphonic oral culture of African America. This identification is also reflected in the formal arrangement of the piece, determining its structural form from beginning to end. Morrison opens the Lecture with the opening phrases of the oral tale, and also brings it to a conclusion in the old woman's response to the children. Formally speaking, therefore, there is nothing in this Lecture which falls outside its framing within the oral tale. This formal arrangement alone would seem to imply that there is nothing in the Lecture in terms of its content, which is intended to be read outside its framing within the oral tale.

Whilst Morrison clearly identifies dead language with both racism and modern Western culture in this Lecture, therefore, she expressly locates living language in the oral cultural forms of Black America. Paradoxically, this means that, despite all the talk about white ideology as a dominant form of language, the dominant ideological perspective presented here is actually that of black language. Moreover, the emphatic valorization of the epistemological and ethical foundations of living language, which is em-bedded within this piece, means that the "Nobel Lecture" can be read as an unequivocal celebration of black language, time, and identity.

Conclusion

Writing on black identity in the US has always been subject to articulation within the comparative framework of Anglo-American and African Ameri-can cultural, political, and epistemological traditions. The most famous for-mulation of this bi-cultural perspective is probably encapsulated in W.E.B. Du Bois's account of "double consciousness," which he defined as:

> a peculiar sensation [...] of always looking at one's self through the eyes of others, of measuring one's soul by the tape of a world that looks on in amused contempt and pity. One ever feels his two-ness, – an American, a Negro; two souls, two thoughts, two unreconciled strivings; two warring ideals in one dark body, whose dogged strength alone keeps it from being torn asunder. (5)

Morrison has spent most of her career explicitly engaged in the struggle to articulate black identity in the context of a dominant and encircling white culture. Despite the wider dissemination of critical analysis on the subject of race to which Morrison has contributed, however, and official initiatives designed to promote multiculturalism as a new social norm, she continues to insist that racism is an issue that defies resolution.[12] She stated in an interview in 2012, for example, that racism is a "cancer which is latent in America" ("Talking Books"). This suggests, in fact, that nothing has really changed since 1989, when she said that "'race' is still a virtually unspeakable thing," a subject that even "genuinely intellectual exchange cannot accommodate" ("Unspeakable" 3).

Morrison plays on the term "unspeakable" here not just to express moral aversion to racism, but to suggest that racist ideology actually resists attempts made by "intellectual exchange" to dismantle its structures. Her own work demonstrates that racialized language functions as a totalizing ideology. For instance, she sums up the conceptual impasse, which total immersion within the language of a dominant ideology presents to the enslaved or colonized subject, in the following description of the fate of Friday in *Robinson Crusoe*:

> it is not just easy to speak the master's language, it is necessary. One is obliged to cooperate in the misuse of figurative language, in the reinforcement of cliché, the erasure of difference, the jargon of justice, the evasion of logic, the denial of history, the crowning of patriarchy, the inscription of hegemony; [...] Such rhetorical strategies become necessary because, without one's own idiom, there is no other language to speak. (*Race-ing* xxviii–ix)

Morrison acknowledged the acute personal and existential difficulties she faced as a writer living and working in the context of a highly racialized language, when she described herself as "a black writer struggling with and through a language that can powerfully evoke and enforce hidden signs of racial superiority, cultural hegemony, and dismissive "othering" of people and language" (*Playing* x–xi).

Given the conclusions of the analysis presented here, however, it seems that her adoption of a temporal perspective on cultural forms may have provided her with a foothold, outside the totalizing structures of racialized language, from which to articulate African American identity as a "center of the self" rather than as the object of another people's discourse ("Unspeakable" 9). She certainly draws on insights provided by the implicit temporal ordering of her philosophy of language to pinpoint the para-

---

[12] The following statement implies that Morrison sees the politics of multiculturalism as little more than a re-inscription of racial inequality: "We need to think about what it means and what it takes to live in a redesigned racial house and and—evasively and erroneously—call it diversity or multiculturalism as a way of calling it home" ("Home" 8).

digmatically critical sources of disparities between the forms of cultural logic which characterize black and white language practices, and their associated perceptions of identity.

It would also seem to be the case that these insights have allowed her to celebrate black identity without reverting to the kind of "racial metaphysics" which simply inverts the current balance of power (Gilroy, *Black Atlantic* 191). This is undoubtedly a danger which she wishes to avoid, as the following comment, from *Playing in the Dark*, illustrates:

> I do not want to alter one hierarchy in order to insinuate another. [...] I do not want to encourage those totalizing approaches to African-American scholarship which have no drive other than the exchange of dominations—dominant Eurocentric scholarship *replaced* by dominant Afrocentric scholarship. (8, emphasis in original)

Temporal modeling can therefore be seen to have provided Morrison with an analytical framework which captures the mechanisms through which racism functions as an essentializing discourse. The very same framework also allows her to describe African American language and culture in terms of a generic, rather than a genetic paradigm of identity, which exhibits a more open sensibility of temporal and linguistic forms. This supports an ethical understanding of alterity, based not on the foundation of an essentialist ontology of being but on a relational model, which tolerates epistemological ambiguity and values individual difference. As a consequence, she can characterize African American cultural forms in terms of a philosophy of language and an ethics of identity which actually resist the essentialist foundations of racially oppressive discourse.

Works Cited

Bakhtin, M.M. *The Dialogic Imagination: Four Essays by M.M. Bakhtin*. Austin, TX: University of Texas Press, 1981.

Bakhtin, M.M. *Speech Genres and Other Late Essays*. Austin, TX: U of Texas P, 1986.

Bhabha, Homi K. *The Location Of Culture*. London: Routledge, 1994.

Christian, Barbara. The Race for Theory." *Within the Circle: An Anthology of African American Literary Criticism from the Harlem Renaissance to the Present*. Ed. Angelyn Mitchell. Durham: Duke UP, 1994.

Christians, Yvette. *Toni Morrison: An Ethical Poetics*. New York: Fordham UP, 2013.

Du Bois, W.E.B. *The Souls of Black Folk*. London: Penguin Books, 1996.

Fanon, Frantz. *Black Skins, White Masks*. London: Pluto, 1986.

Gilroy, Paul. *The Black Atlantic: Modernity and Double Consciousness*. Cambridge, Massachusetts: Harvard UP, 1993.

Gilroy, Paul. *Small Acts: Thoughts on the Politics of Black Cultures*. London: Serpent's Tail, 1993.

Hegel, Georg Wilhelm Friedrich. *The Philosophy of History*. New York: Dover Publications, 1956.

Lubiano, Wahneema, ed. *The House That Race Built: Black Americans, U.S. Terrain*. New York: Pantheon Books, 1997.

Mitchell, Angelyn, ed. *Within the Circle: An Anthology of African American Literary Criticism from the Harlem Renaissance to the Present*. Durham: Duke UP, 1994.

Morrison, Toni. "Writers Together." *Nation* 24 Oct. 1981: 396–397, 412.

—. "Memory, Creation and Writing." *Thought* Vol. 59, No. 235 (Dec. 1984): 385–390.

—. *Beloved* London: Picador, 1988.

—. "Unspeakable Things Unspoken: The African American Presence in American Literature." *Michigan Quarterly Review* Vol. 28, No. 1 (1989): 1–34.

—. *Playing in the Dark: Whiteness and the Literary Imagination*. Cambridge: Harvard UP, 1992.

—. ed. *Race-ing Justice, En-gendering Power: Essays on Anita Hill, Clarence Thomas, and the Construction of Social Reality*. London: Chatto & Windus, 1993.

—. "Home." *The House That Race Built: Black Americans, U.S. Terrain*. Ed. Wahneema Lubiano. New York: Pantheon Books, 1997. 3–12.

—. "The Future of Time: Literature and Diminished Expectations." *What Moves at the Margin: Selected Nonfiction*. Jackson: UP of Mississippi, 2008. 170–86.

—. "The Nobel Lecture in Literature." *What Moves at the Margin: Selected Nonfiction*. Jackson: UP of Mississippi, 2008. 198–207.

—. *What Moves at the Margin: Selected Nonfiction*. Jackson: UP of Mississippi, 2008.

—. "Interview with Razia Iqbal." *Talking Books* BBC News, 5 October, 2012. Extract available at http:www.bbc.co.uk/news/world-radio-and-tv-19834043. Retrieved 13/09/13.

Rice, Alan. *Radical Narratives of the Black Atlantic*. Continuum, 2003.

Said, Edward. *Orientalism*. London: Penguin, 2003.

Toni Morrison's *The Bluest Eye*:
Lost and Found in Translation

Lynn Penrod

When marking the thirtieth anniversary of the awarding of the Nobel Prize in Literature to Toni Morrison, most of us have absolutely no difficulty in understanding the choice of the Nobel Prize Committee of 1993. Morrison, to quote her Nobel citation, is a writer, "who in novels characterized by visionary force and poetic import, gives life to an essential aspect of American reality" (Nobelprize.org). But here we also come to some critical questions for the literary translator of a Nobel laureate's work. What happens to an author's work, either the entire body of work, or perhaps just a single book, when it appears "in translation"? And, more particularly, what is the translational fate of any writer in the wake of becoming forever known as "Nobel Prize-winning author X"? [1]

When a Nobel laureate is known primarily, often solely, through a body of work that has originally appeared in a language other than English (prime recent examples would include Elfriede Jelinek, Herta Müller, Orhan Pahmuk, Mo Yan, or Tomas Tranströmer), the result is predictably an instantaneous deluge of demands from English-speaking readers desperately seeking translations of these authors' works. Literary translators worldwide work feverishly to meet publishers' deadlines. Online booksellers and independent booksellers alike to provide rush copies (often branded with special stickers declaring "Winner of the Nobel Prize" or quickly given new dust jackets with the words "Nobel Prize Winner" emblazoned on them). Publishers can be fairly sure that sales will increase, perhaps not

---

[1] This essay provides only a very general introduction to a planned larger study dealing with Nobel laureates in literature and their translation profiles before and after winning the Nobel Prize. It is intended to encourage the translation of Nobel laureates into as many world languages as possible.

forever, but certainly sufficiently to ensure at least a small increase in their bottom line. For literary scholars as well, the announcement of a new Nobel laureate is also a source of new and exciting possibilities for research and translation plays a critical role here. And for the reading public (from members of book clubs to travelers seeking a 'good read' on a train or plane) the Nobel Prize for Literature serves as a reliable assurance that their reading experience will be if not always enjoyable at least thought-provoking.

So what do we mean when we speak of "Toni Morrison in translation"? What actually happens to her work (or indeed the work of any writer) as it crosses not only linguistic borders but entire cultural frontiers as well? How do the theory and practice of "translating" Toni Morrison's novels potentially affect Morrison criticism, analysis, reputation, or pedagogy?

What is "Found" in Translation?

I should perhaps begin by defining what I mean by literary translation. And what does the process of literary translation allow us to "find" in a writer's work? Rainer Schulte, co-founder of the American Literary Translators Association, has stated:

> Literary translation bridges the delicate emotional connections between cultures and languages and furthers the understanding of human beings across national borders. In the act of literary translation, the soul of another culture becomes transparent, and the translator recreates the refined sensibilities of foreign countries and their people through the linguistic, musical, rhythmic, and visual possibilities of the new language. (UTDallas.edu)

While Schulte may be overly optimistic about the reality of what literary translation can offer, it is important to remember that simply in terms of the importance and dissemination of any author's work, translation has always played an integral part in establishing reputation, longevity, acceptance into the literary canon of world literature, or increased scholarly attention to any individual work or writer.

That said, however, the place of translation within the literary system was for many centuries limited to a secondary role, translation being considered the handmaiden of literature and translators mere technicians whose goal was to provide equivalence of the linguistic text, thereby transporting the original (creative) text into an equivalent (but not creative in the sense of an "original" author's creativity) version, thus making the author's work accessible to a larger global reading public.

In very general terms literary translation can be considered somewhat arbitrarily as involving two major overlapping areas of intellectual endeavor: the linguistic and the cultural. One must never forget, however, that for a translator these two discourses, linguistic and cultural, are constantly in dialogue. Although the majority of early prominent scholars dealing with translation came largely from the field of linguistics (Georges Mounin, Eugene Nida, Jiri Levy, M.B. Dagut, Albrecht Neubert, for example), later contributors to what has become over the course of the past three decades a new discipline within the humanities, Translation Studies, focus their work on the importance of culture within the translation process.

Roman Jakobson speaks of three major types of translation: intralingual (re-wording), interlingual (what he terms translation proper), and inter-semiotic (transmutation, or moving from verbal to non-verbal sign systems) and like other linguists points out that complete equivalence is always impossible (Jakobson, 237). Yet Octavio Paz, in his essay "Translation: Literature and Letters," refers to translation as a confirmation and guarantee of spiritual bonds (Schulte and Biguenet, 152). Because we are able to translate, there must be some sort of underlying spiritual structure that allows us to do it. Yet Paz points out as well that translation eventually becomes, or can become, a tool for the exploitation of differences rather than common ground between people from different places. He also underscores the fact that languages are significantly nation bound, stating that "the language that enables us to communicate with one another also encloses us in an invisible web of sounds and meanings, so that each nation is imprisoned by its language, a language further fragmented by historical eras, by social classes, by generations" (153).

Thus we see that although cultural issues and context have always been important features of translation (an activity that has been going on even before the Tower of Babel), the primary focus of a translation began as solidly grounded in linguistic 'equivalence' and for many practicing translators remains so today. However, Paz's words lead us to that more recent focus of translation studies scholars, the insistence on what we call "the cultural turn" in translation, which is critical for any study of Toni Morrison's work in translation. Without going into great detail about the evolution of this "cultural turn," let's use an illustrative example provided by Susan Bassnett in her *Reflections on Translation*:

> An English teacher from New Zealand told me about the difficulty she had convincing her pupils that the poetry they were reading about spring

35

happening in April made sense. In Northern Europe, the daffodils do start to flower in March and by April, spring is so advanced that Browning could write longingly about wanting to be back in England at that most beautiful time of the year. But in the southern hemisphere the daffodils bloom in September, while in April the leaves are falling and winter is on the way. How then to understand the symbolic significance of T. S. Eliot's lines "April is the cruelest month breeding/Lilacs out of the dead land" or Shakespeare's ironic "men are April when they woo" without engaging in what can only be called cultural translation? (Bassnett, *Reflections* 124–25)

This example dealing with seasons is only one of many that punctuate the importance, increasingly so, of literary translation despite the calls for global English or ELF (English as the world's *lingua franca*). But given that Morrison writes both within a western tradition and in English, why does the cultural turn matter so much in translations of her work?

Susan Huddleston Edgerton, in her article, "Remembering the mother tongue(s): Toni Morrison, Julie Dash and the language of pedagogy," emphasizes that a crucial theme in all of Morrison's work involves memory and the importance of translating the (body) memory. Edgerton is here speaking as if "translation" were a kind of higher-level metaphor; however, if one considers the cultural significance of Toni Morrison's work as that of giving voice to "American reality," it is not difficult to understand the intimate connection between translation as metaphor and literary translation as cultural process in action. This connection can be seen not only in the re-production of Morrison's "English" text in another language but in another culture as well. As Edgerton states:

> Memory involves a kind of translation, an ongoing reinterpretation of events, thoughts, feelings, and sensations past. Remembering is translation within a body, though it is mediated by a community of listeners, or imagined listeners, and by time. Its utterance sometimes emerges as testimony, sometimes confession, revelation, complaint, nostalgia, or ordinary conversation. Translation memory to language can be rich or poor, revisionary or compulsive. (…) Translation, memory, and testimony surely operate somewhere in between. (342)

Translation of literary texts concerns the crossing of linguistic as well as cultural, economic, and historical barriers effectively. Translating Toni Morrison provides the literary translator with an interesting set of challenges indeed.

Toni Morrison "Found" and "Lost" in Translation: The Case of The Bluest Eye
As already suggested, the Nobel Prize marks the moment in the career of a writer when many publishers, scholars, and readers worldwide discover him or her either for the first time or in a more comprehensive manner. The very best accolade of the Nobel Prize in Literature is often neither the monetary prize nor a nation's pride that one of its authors has been honored. It is rather the possibility of an introduction to and appreciation of new ideas, new situations, and new narrative worlds previously unexplored. When searching for information about available translations of a Nobel laureate's literary works, most literary translators use World Cat as their common reference tool. However, it is often the case that translations are not easily located using ordinary search tools. In the case of Toni Morrison's *The Bluest Eye*, World Cat provides the following information relating to translations into various languages since its publication in 1970: Japanese (3), Spanish (3), German (2), Persian (2), Turkish (2), and one each in Chinese, Czech, Danish, Dutch, Finnish, French, Hebrew, Italian, Korean, Norwegian, Portuguese, Slovak, Slovenian, and Vietnamese.[2]

In the introduction to his guide to *The Bluest Eye*, Harold Bloom gives us an important insight into the text when he states that "Morrison's story is a powerful dramatic expression of the sentiment conveyed by James Baldwin in his essay, 'Autobiographical Notes':"

> I don't think that the Negro problem in America can even be discussed coherently without bearing in mind its context; its context being the history, traditions, customs, the moral assumptions and preoccupations of the country; in short, the general social fabric. Appearances to the contrary, no one in America escapes its effects and everyone in America bears some responsibility for it. (*Notes of a Native Son*, 1955, quoted in Bloom, 20)

What does this mean for a translator of *The Bluest Eye*? Given that the two languages I work in are English and French, I can use the French translation of Morrison's text in order to describe how the two intertwined facets of

---

[2] Other translations of Morrison's works into French include *Sula*, trans. P. Alien, Paris, Bourgois, 1992; *Le Chant de Salomon*, trans. S. Rué, Paris, Acropole, Collection 10/18, 1985; retrans. J. Guiloineau, Paris, Bourgois, 1996 ; *Tar Baby*, tr. S. Rué, Paris, Acropole, Collection 10/18, 1986; trans. J. Guiloineau, Paris, Bourgois, 1996. *Beloved*, trans. H. Chabrier and S. Rué, Paris, Bourgois, Collection 10/18, 1986 ; *Jazz*, trans. P. Alien, Paris, Bourgois, 1992. The largest number of Morrison's translations were published in 1994, one year following the awarding of the 1993 Nobel Prize for Literature.

translation, the linguistic and the cultural, provide major challenges in the important task of moving Toni Morrison narrative world from American English into French. The discussion that follows does not have as its object the evaluation of the French translation; indeed it is for the most part a good one and many of the linguistic and cultural challenges have been met adequately by Morrison's French translator. My objective is to make Morrison scholars, whatever their language, aware of the Toni Morrison created through translation and to underscore the necessity of appropriate cultural as well as linguistic knowledge bases for the translator.

The only French translation of *The Bluest Eye* (*L'Oeil le plus bleu*) was published in Paris in 1994, one year following the writer's Nobel Prize, by Christian Bourgois and translated by Jean Guiloineau, a well-respected translator who is probably best known for his French translations of works related to Nelson Mandela and South Africa. When Guiloineau was asked in a 2011 interview why he had decided to translate the novel, he responded that it had not been his idea originally but that he had been approached by the publisher and had accepted since he considers Morrison to be one of America's greatest writers.

Asked what his impressions were after a first reading of the novel, Guiloineau answered:

> The first reading presented numerous problems in terms of translation. The first novel by Toni Morrison seemed to me to be rather different from those I had already read (*Sula, Beloved, Tar Baby*...) The special world of childhood, narrated incidents of violence and tenderness, a kind of contained rage linked to the situation of Blacks (...) I had to put all that into French with the same grace, the same elegance as Toni Morrison's writing. The fact that I had not already read the novel (...) helped me. I was "new" in a way in terms of this novel and in terms of Morrison's work. (Elsa et Léa, np) [my translation]

Guiloineau goes on to state that although he later met Morrison (and went on to translate another work by her), his relationship with her was never particularly warm. It is also of note that this is a translation from the Hexagon, metropolitan France, and has perhaps not had as wide a dissemination or distribution in other francophone countries, as one would hope for—where Morrison's texts (not only *The Bluest Eye*, but many others) would perhaps have greater resonance since readers there, both in terms of their past colonial relationship to France as well as their postcolonial contemporary dealings with things French, would be eager to explore a similar terrain set in America.

Guiloineau does make clear that Morrison's work exists within a very particular context: the narrative of slavery, the struggle for human rights in the United States, the sometimes specific sub-cultures of jazz or blues. Her language is particularly powerful and evocative, demonstrating a mastery of English "with a touch of poetry" and an ability to play with various types of American "Englishes" to show differences in class, history, and culture between not only Whites and Blacks but between North and South as well. To make all this accessible to the French reader, using only the resources of the French language, which of course has had an entirely different history, is an enormous challenge.

Linguistic and Cultural Challenges for Translators of The Bluest Eye

Even though *The Bluest Eye* is Morrison's first novel, it nonetheless provides a vast inventory of her incredibly creative and musical use of Africanisms and Afro-American English within an American context of several historical time periods—the 40s, the 60s, and even earlier.

But simply to begin at the beginning, the translator must make a very important initial decision about translation of the title: *The Bluest Eye*. In French the translator has simply kept the original, opting for a singular eye (*L'Oeil le plus bleu*). Yet the Spanish translators have opted for the plural, *Ozos azules*. The bluest "eye" is of course, not precisely what Pecola has wished for: she wants blue eyes, the symbol of everything "beautiful" in the white world to which she does not belong. Yet Morrison has carefully chosen a singular "Eye" for her title as it is the homonym of the English first-person singular, *I*, pronoun of identity formation and agency, a loss in any other language.

Questions of register and the complex interweaving and cross-cutting of time and place in Morrison's text also present significant linguistic challenges to the translator throughout the text. The voices of the child Claudia and the adult Claudia, although belonging to the same character, must be heard differently. "Quiet as it's kept" (np), "Nuns go by as quiet as lust" (9), or the difference between "being put out and being put out*doors*" (17)— these sound like fairly basic English phrases, but for the translator they represent many hours of thoughtful consideration and attention.

These days, literary translators, balancing competing concepts of localization and 'foreignization', tend to leave place names and character names in their original language. However, it is nonetheless interesting to ponder how the non-English reader will react to the names Cholly Breedlove, Soaphead Church, or Pecola, or whether Lorain, Ohio; Mobile, Alabama; or Macon, Georgia can successfully carry the resonance of place into French that is so carefully communicated in Morrison's English text.

The skin color spectrum so artfully deployed by Morrison in *The Bluest Eye* is also a potential minefield of challenges: "high-yellow dream girl" (62), "sugar-brown" (82), or "love, thick and dark as Alaga syrup" (12) are just a few examples of critical vocabulary a translator must come to terms with. The use of common Afro-American speech rhythms and pronunciations [the insults hurled at Pecola: "Black e mo" or "Ya daddsleeps nekked"(65); the concept of "playing nasty" (30); "six-finger-dog-tooth-meringue-pie"(73); "You'd make a haint buy a girdle" (52); or the McTeer girls' worry that "mama gone get us" (105)] must be carefully and consistently handled.

While on this purely linguistic level the translator of any of Morrison's texts faces a difficult yet rewarding task, beyond the linguistic elements that threaten the text's integrity as it crosses frontiers from English into "other-than-English" we need to consider the cultural divide separating the American Lorain, Ohio, of *The Bluest Eye* from the receiving cultural landscape of the unilingual French reader in Paris, Tunis, or Martinique. And perhaps the best example of the very large cultural translation problem for the translator of *The Bluest Eye* is the lengthy primer passage that begins the text. I quote it here in its entirety, admitting that it is not necessarily much of a linguistic challenge but that arguably it stands as a Mount Everest of cultural translation challenge that I believe has proved impossible to conquer for any translator to date.

> Here is the house. It is green and white. It has a red door. It is very pretty. Here is the family. Mother, Father, Dick, and Jane live in the green-and-white house. They are very happy. See Jane. She has a red dress. She wants to play. Who will play with Jane? See the cat. It goes meow-meow. Come and play. Come and play with Jane. The kitten will not play. See Mother. Mother is very nice. Mother, will you play with Jane? Mother laughs. Laugh, Mother, laugh. See Father. He is big and strong. Father, will you play with Jane? Father is smiling. Smile, Father, smile. See the dog. Bowwow goes the dog. Do you want to play with Jane? See the dog run. Run, dog, run. Look, look. Here comes a friend. The friend will play with Jane. They will play a good game. Play, Jane, play. (Morrison 1970, 3)

Many critics and interpreters of *The Bluest Eye* have commented extensively on these generic yet instantly recognizable excerpts from the very well-known (at least to American readers) series of primers from which many of us learned to read. William Elson and William Gray's Dick and Jane stories, so familiar to American children who were of school-age in the 1940s through the late 1960s, are incredibly culturally rooted. The Elson-Gray primers originated in the 1930s and became extremely popular through the 1940s and 1950s. With their idealized middle-class family of three children (Dick, Jane, and little sister Sally), a dog (Spot) and a cat (Puff), they reproduce existing class and race divergence and reinforce dominant ideologies of the day.

The friction between the picture of the American dream presented in the primers is extraordinarily hard to handle without resorting to extra-textual material such as a translator's introduction or a set of translator's notes relating to many of the culturally significant elements of Morrison's text. Not only are the primer excerpts repeated as a kind of preface to the textual narrative, they also serve as prefaces to the various narrative threads throughout the novel, and we can easily see how Morrison "illuminates disparities between the primer's representations and the realities of life for black children. By running the words of the primer together, she shows the redundancy of this 'definitive' narrative of childhood" (Lister, 26). Yet the ordinary practice of contemporary publishers of translations is to reject a translator's attempts (via an introduction or translator's notes) to provide essential cultural context for a book, even when that context is critical for a reader's full appreciation of the text.

Other cultural references within *The Bluest Eye*, whether to Shirley Temple dolls or cups, Mary Jane candies, the film *Imitation of Life*, while perhaps not linguistic challenges, still leave the translator often searching for innovative ways to supplement the text so that readers who have no knowledge of these cultural artifacts, will understand or at least be curious enough to find out about them.

Conclusion, Or Why Translation Matters

In a moving and memorable speech upon her acceptance of the National Book Foundation's Medal for Distinguished Contribution to American letters in 1996, Toni Morrison relates two anecdotes, one about a "reader disabled by an absence of solitude" and the other about a "writer imperiled by the absence of a hospitable community," stating that both stories "fuse and underscore ...the seriousness of the industry whose sole purpose is the publication of writers for readers" (Morrison, *Dancing* 15–16). I would simply suggest here that we add *translator* to reader and *writer* as a focus of

Morrison's concern related to the seriousness of the publishing industry in the twenty-first century. Without translation the publishing industry, even the virtual publishing industry, cannot thrive.

When asked by interviewer Thomas Le Clair for her opinion of what makes her own work "good," Morrison replied:

> The language, only the language. The language must be careful and must appear effortless. It must not sweat. It must suggest and be provocative at the same time. It is the thing that black people love so much—the saying of words, holding them on the tongue, experimenting with them, playing with them. It's a love, a passion. Its function is like a preacher's: to make you stand up out of your seat, make you lose yourself and hear yourself. The worst of all possible things that could happen would be to lose that language. There are certain things I cannot say without recourse to my language. It's terrible to think that a child with five different present tenses comes to school to be faced with those books that are less than his own language. And then to be told things about his language, which is him, that are sometimes permanently damaging. He may never know the etymology of Africanisms in this language, or even know that "hip" is really a word or that "the dozens" meant something. This is a really cruel fallout of racism. I know the standard English. I want to use it to help restore the other language, the lingua franca. (Morrison quoted in Le Clair, 27)

In a recent interview on National Public Radio, Edith Grossman, award-winning Spanish-to-English literary translator, had this to say: "I think translation is the cement that holds literary civilization together. It's the way we learn about other literatures, other peoples (…). The way we learn about the world is through translation. Since not everyone can read every language in the world, the only way to find out what people are writing and thinking is to read translations" (NPR).

Toni Morrison has often been quoted on why she began writing and in several speeches has told her audience that if there is a book that you want to read but that has not yet been written you must be the one to write it. For literary translators Morrison's message could easily be modified to state that if there is a book that you want others to read but that has not been translated, you must be the one to translate it—or at the very least encourage another translator to find a willing publisher, take on the task, and in that way allow the writer's narrative world to be shared by others.

For Edith Grossman there are two qualities that mark a good translation and two fundamental questions to be answered. First of all, does reading the translation move you to find out more about the original author and their work? And secondly, do you forget that it's a translation and simply become involved in the fiction or the poem that you're reading? "In a way," says Grossman, "those two things move in opposite directions—one towards the original and the other towards the end result of the translation" (NPR).

I would love to think that *The Bluest Eye* could be read, would be read, by ever so many readers, not simply because Toni Morrison is a Nobel Prize winner but because her novels provide such a provocative and rich examination of lived existence in times and places that we must continue to explore. Coming to the works of Toni Morrison not as a specialist but rather as a reader and translator, I can only hope that raising the level of awareness of the importance and critical role of literary translation in relation to her work, I will have achieved my objective.

The words of Trudier Harris from 1994 have indeed proved to be prophetic:

> Morrison's winning of the Nobel Prize in Literature, therefore, was the official inscription of a worldwide recognition and appreciation of the intellectual stimulation and awesome power of her writing. As probably the most well-known of African American writers and perhaps even of all contemporary American writers, Morisson has provided for inter-national readers an entrée into American culture and specifically into African America culture. (...) The Nobel Prize in literature will mean that Morrison's works will be ever more popular and ever more available (Harris, 10).

Morrison's popularity is certainly well established. The global availability of her works in translation, however, still requires our attention.

Works Cited

Barstow, Jane Missner. "At the Intersection: Race, Culture, Identity, and the Aesthetics in *The Bluest Eye*." Print.

Bassnett, Susan, and André Lefevere, eds. *Translation, History and Culture*. London and NewYork: Pinter Publishers, 1990. Print.

Bassnett, Susan. *Reflections on Translation*. Toronto: Multilingual Matters, 2011. Print.

—. *Translation Studies*. New York: Routledge, 2002. Print.

Bloom, Harold. *Bloom's Guides: Toni Morrison's "The Bluest Eye."* New York: Infobase, 2010. Print.

Brower, R.A., ed. *On Translation.* Cambridge: Harvard UP, 1959. Print.

Carlacio, Jami L., ed. The Fiction of Toni Morrison. Reading and Writing on Race, Culture, and Identity. Urbana, Illinois: National Council of Teachers of English, 2007. Print.

Edgerton, Susan Huddleston. "Re-membering the Mother Tongue(s): Toni Morrison, Julie Dash and the Language of Pedagogy." *Cultural Studies* 9:2 (1995): 338–363. Print.

Elsa et Léa. "Entretien avec Jean Guiloineau, traducteur." *Traduction*, 14 January 2011. Web. 29 June 2013.

Harris, Trudier. "Toni Morrison: Solo Flight through Literature into History." *World Literature Today*, 68:1 (1994): 9–14. Print.

Jakobson, Roman. "On Linguistic Aspects of Translation." In *On Translation*. Vol 3, 1959: 30–39.

Le Clair, Thomas. "The Language Must Not Sweat." *New Republic*, 21 March 1981: 25–29. Web. 20 Aug 2013.

Lister, Rachel. *Reading Toni Morrison.* Denver: Greenwood, 2009. Print.

Morrison, Toni. *The Bluest Eye.* 1970. New York: Vintage. Print.

—. Foreword. *The Bluest Eye.* 1993. New York: Vintage. Print.

—. *L'Oeil le plus bleu.* Trans. Jean Guiloineau. Paris: Christian Bourgois, 1994. Print.

—. *The Dancing Mind.* New York: Knopf, 1996. Print.

National Public Radio. "Five Books: Edith Grossman on Translation." 29 December 2012. Web. 6 July 2013.

Nobelprize.org. Web. 10 Aug. 2013.

Royon, Tessa. *The Cambridge Introduction to Toni Morisson.* Cambridge: Cambridge UP, 2013. Print.

Schulte, Rainer, and John Biguenet, eds. *Theories of Translation: An Anthology of Essays from Dryden to Derrida.* Chicago: U of Chicago P, 1992. Print.

UTDallas.edu. American Literary Translators Association (ALTA). Web. 4 May 2013.

Teaching Toni Morrison to a Culturally Diverse Class: Experiences from Bangladesh

Sangita Rayamajhi

The Asian University for Women (AUW) in Bangladesh is a university where young women students from more than a dozen countries are educated with an objective to become women leaders in their communities. The university is a place where the histories and experiences of collective memory and social, structural and political inequality are constantly being challenged and re-defined. The multicultural setting within the classroom is a pastiche of histories, histories which have collided and colluded, of religious dogmatism which refuse to unravel or 'unbelieve' the historical beliefs.

In such a setting I introduced Toni Morrison and her first multi-cultural book *The Bluest Eye*. With Morrison there is no clear-cut answer to any of the questions regarding her intricately complex works. By discussing issues and concerns about Pecola and the world she lives in, I draw similarities with the general beliefs and practices in Asia. This essay is not a compara-tive study between the literatures or texts of America and Asia. It is more of a cultural commentary while I attempt to draw Pecola and her community out of that world and situate them in an altogether different locale and see if they function as brilliantly as they do in their own space. This essay at-tempts to see how *The Bluest Eye* was perceived by the class at the Asian University for Women in Bangladesh and how well the idioms, the nuances and the dynamics of the African American community were recognized as 'almost' their own.

This book was introduced in the World Literature Class. The students, twenty-five in all, were of various cultural backgrounds and religious beliefs. The course was not a comparative study of West and East. The intention was to make sure the students were able to understand the idioms of African American writings and see if they could relate to them. They had

45

been reading works on minorities, on untouchables, outcastes, tribals, and marginalized women. During the first day of class on Morrison, one student commented, "How is it that the violence and victimization that pervades our part of the world is evident as much in Morrison's work? Is she not American?" This question led me to try to contextualize the colonial legacy and Orientalist notions that Morrison engages in her work.

Contextualizing the Colonial Legacy

Colonial discourse is one topic of discussion that comes up repeatedly in world literature. Many of the students are from countries where they have directly or indirectly inherited the legacy of colonization so that it is not very difficult to make them capture the nuances and eccentricities of the colonial world. For every post-colonial writer it is not so much the vision of the present-future psycho-social and cultural dynamics that is of importance. The post-colonial critic Homi Bhabha suggests that, remembering 'is never a quiet act of introspection or retrospection. It is a painful remembering, a putting together of the dismembered past to make sense of the trauma of the present' (Bhabha 63). In *The Bluest Eye,* through the painful experience of Pecola, Morrison delineates the impact colonization has had on African American community.

In Asia the cultural context of colonization was built on the idea of the Orient, "an ideology of racism which upheld white norms as standard and denigrated our deviance from them" (Tharu 256). Adhering to those White-initiated socio-cultural norms can, and have proven to be destructive to the native people in many ways. The colonial presence has given rise to tortuous psycho-cultural situations to the once colonized peoples. Clothes, food habits, and primarily language and literature and their uses, still cause a great deal of embarrassment to intellectuals, even today. "In writing the 'Orient' through certain governing metaphors and tropes, Orientalists simultaneously underwrote the 'positional superiority' of Western consciousness and, in so doing, rendered the 'Orient' a playground for Western 'desire, repressions, investments, projections'" (Said, *Orientalism* 8). The literature that subsequently arose was a literary sub-culture that owed its very existence to the colonial presence. And the culture that arose had to come to terms with the environment it grew against, so that the existing social, economic and political structures were undermined:

> British Imperialists justified its continued, and after 1857, militaristic presence in India (both to its own liberal conscience and to our muted

questioning) through an elaborately developed ideology of racism, designed to prove Indians (especially the urban upper castes) as weak and immoral, incapable of just government. Imperial presence was projected as necessary, benign, restraining, parental. Obviously this ideology helped entrench colonial presence by convincing the colonized of their fundamental inhumanity and the consequent need for the colonizer's permanent presence. (Tharu 257)

In *The Bluest Eye*, Morrison prefaces the story with a paragraph from a children's book with a family of "Mother, Father, Dick and Jane," white characters out of a seemingly "green-and-white house" (1). The paragraph poses a challenge to the oft-repeated white world of the White people depicted either in children's stories or the grown-up world of Morrison's time. The colonizing effects of White female beauty upon a black girl and her community, is painted with excruciating beauty. Thus we see the psycho-social image of the 'white is beautiful' belief that is inherited from the White colonizers, and which in turn gives rise to the text which for Morrison was, in a way, to decolonize the black psyche. Pecola's life is open to the whims of those people who were introduced to western tradition, including her own mother. At every step of her life she is faced with attitudes and images based on the myth of white superiority, which leads her to self-hatred. Pecola's reflections of herself is an example of the self-image she inherited.

> It had occurred to Pecola some time ago that if her eyes, those eyes that held the pictures, and knew the sights—if those eyes of hers were different, that is to say beautiful, she herself would be different. Her teeth were good, and at least her nose was not big and flat like some of those who were thought so cute. If she looked different, and Mrs. Breedlove too. Maybe they'd say, "why look at pretty-eyed Pecola. We mustn't do bad things in front of those pretty eyes." (46)

In both Western and Asian cultures outer good looks are considered to be the reflection of inner beauty. In Asia, furthermore the fairness of the skin is synonymous to being beautiful. In South Asia there is an increasing popularity of *Fair and Lovely*, a face cream promising to turn your dark skin into a fair and lovely one. This television advertisement is the inheritance of the colonized mind which continues to believe that to be dark is to be ugly, a valorization of what one cannot be. Many Asians still suffer from a low sense of self-esteem due to the internalization of the colonial culture.

Similarly, "Pecola's desire for blue eyes reflects a community absorbed by white ideas of what is beautiful. References to idols of white female beauty, Greta Garbo, Ginger Rogers, Jean Harlow, and to the child icon of beauty, Shirley Temple, bespeak an obsession with a standard of white female beauty, that, in turn renders black women and girls invisible" (Pereira 74). This repressive behavior of disowning the signifiers of the self in both the cultures may, as Patrice Comier Hamilton says, lead to "following an unhealthy path of self-hatred rather than self love" (116), which is the case with Pecola.

Caste and Class: Pecola and Velutha

Recalling Velutha, a social outcaste in Arundhati Roy's *God of Small Things,* Pecola is deprived of social identity. Pecola is placed in the identifiable margin of the class structure in a society of Whites and the Blacks. Velutha is a social 'other' due to his caste, his identity (or lack of it) as an 'untouchable.' Pecola yearns to be loved by her own mother Pauline and accepted by her friends and neighbors who are White. Abused and unrecognized for who she is, she careens into madness. Velutha falls in love with Ammu, a woman of a superior caste and class, a location to which he cannot cross over. He dies, defiled and waiting for that love to be recognized by the rest of Ammu's family. It never happens.

The hierarchy of class and caste are well recognized by the students at Asian University for Women, since it is a part of their life's conditioning and therefore learning. They are aware of its existence and all the characteristics of exclusions and intimidations. *God of Small Things* itself carries autobiographical traits of the writer, a recognition of what was a common practice in the society and continues to be. The social anthropologist Leela Dube classifies class into three basic categories:

> birth status group are exclusion or separation (rules governing marriage and contact, which maintain distinction of caste), hierarchy (the principle of order and rank according to status), and interdependence (the division of labour which is closely tied to hierarchy and separation). These three analytically separable principles of the caste system operate not so much through individuals as through units based on kinship. (467)

In Roy's novel, the family refuses to recognize Velutha and Ammu's relationship only because of the class and caste difference, defined by the abject poverty that Velutha grew up in. Even Velutha's father dreads the relationship. Similarly, Geraldine, "the milk brown lady in the pretty gold and green house," calls her "a nasty little black bitch" because Pecola wore a "dirty torn dress" and "muddy shoes with the wad of gum peeping out from between the cheap soles" because she reeked of poverty and was black (71).

Inside a classroom, it is very important that the students are able to relate to the topics under discussion. And this is not an easy task when the homogeneity of the all-women's class is defied by the socio-cultural and religious diversity. I also became increasingly aware that the colonial burden, which they inherited through oral traditions in their own homes and community, has not yet lifted from the minds of the students. Within the classroom, therefore, Edward Said's theory of blending American racism and European colonialism into one concoction and considering it to be the oppression of the White over the darker-skinned people is seen when parallels are drawn between Pecola suffering from White oppression and the colonized people of Asia.

The Initiation Story

The Bluest Eye, Morrison's first book and in itself an initiation story, describes the coming of age of a little black girl. Pecola's traumatic experience is symptomatic of the terror of the first bleeding, the coming of age by reaching puberty of girls in Asia, especially in South Asia.

> Suddenly Pecola bolted straight up, her eyes wide with terror. A whinnying sound came from her mouth. "What's the matter with *you*?" Frieda stood up too. Then we both looked where Pecola was staring. Blood was running down her legs. Some drops were on the steps. I leaped up. "Hey. You cut yourself? Look. It's all over your dress." A brownish-red stain discolored the back of her dress. She kept whinnying, standing with her legs far apart. Frieda said, "Oh Lordy! I know. I know what that is!" (19)

This first step into womanhood, as it is referred to in most parts of Asia, is indeed traumatic to the young girls because of their lack of knowledge about the situation, since the mothers and elders do not choose to divulge the secrets of womanhood to them. The adults demand respect and do not expect the children especially girls to ask them personal questions about their own body. What Claudia says is so recognizably true in Asia, "Adults do not talk to us—they give us directions. They issue orders without providing information" (13). In other words the conversation is so hierarchically structured that the children do not turn around to question or seek an answer, again as Claudia notes, "It was certainly not for us to 'dispute' her. We didn't initiate talk with grownups; we answered their questions" (23).

In Asia, once the daughter has her first menstruation, she is secluded from society, and is not permitted to go out and play openly with other children of the community or to go out with friends without strictly adhering to restrictions of time and place. As Nadeau and Rayamajhi say, "Mothers become extra watchful when their daughters reach puberty. It is a markedly significant rite of passage in an adolescent woman's life and in Asia, a woman who has reached puberty begins to be closely scrutinized by her mother, family members, and society at large. Thus the transition to womanhood can be difficult" (88).

Therefore, as children, once they understand that the menstruating blood is a signifier of restrictions, it turns out to be very traumatic for the girl as well as for the parents. Since most of the women from AUW are from less privileged strata of the society they were able to identify with the traumatic experience. The family is afraid that their bodies may be physically violated, that they may lose their standing, that it may mar their social status, that the daughter may never get a suitable husband, or a good family for her to get married into. For the characters of Morrison's world and the students of my classroom, the trauma of the first menstruation is the same.

Understanding Violence in The Bluest Eye

Violence, incest and madness are strung together by the central concern of racism in *The Bluest Eye*. The issues that Morrison tackles here are not exotic to the Asian mind. Neither are they unrecognizable. Domestic violence is very common in Asia, especially in Bangladesh, India and Pakistan. Taking the example of Bangladesh, in 2004, the UN published a report on domestic violence in the country depending heavily on newspaper reportage (Immigration and Refugee Board of Canada 2004). Sixty-five per cent of Bangladeshi males think it is justifiable to beat up their wives, 38 percent have no clear idea what constitutes physical violence and 40 percent support keeping women socially dormant (Immigration and Refugee Board of Canada 2004). The same UN report states that another newspaper (*The Independent*) reported that Bangladesh stands second in the world in terms of violence against women in different forms, such as women battering, wife beating, domestic and dowry-related violence, acid attack, rape, physical and verbal harassment, fatwa, work place sexual harassment, trafficking and prostitution, polygamy and child abuse (Immigration and Refugee Board of Canada 2004).

One can take the recent example of the Delhi rape case which created a huge sensation in India and other countries of the South Asian region. On December 16, 2012, a 23-year-old girl was raped by four men in a moving bus in South Delhi. After the incident New Delhi earned the name of "rape capital." This was not a lone case. According to *Hindustan Times* of September 11, 2013, many women filed complaints of being harassed in public places, "and travelling alone especially during the night becomes a nightmare," they said.

Violence within the home is equally prevalent in Asia and as Nadeau and Rayamajhi put it:

> Women are also subjected to a variety of violence in the home, primarily as daughters, sisters, and wives. Some of these violent acts include exchange marriages, marriage to the Quran, marriage to temples, karo-kari (honor killings), bride-price, dowry, female circumcision, child marriage, sex selective abortion, and denial of widow marriages. Again in the Muslim community, a daughter is often forced to swear by the Quran that she would not covet the property of her brothers. Forced prostitution, mainly through the trafficking of girls and women, is also common in the region. (95)

When scenes of violence were discussed in the classroom, the impact it made on these young women was similar to the effect that other Asian literature which deal with violence had on them. For example, *Middle of Silence*, a play by a Sri Lankan playwright Ruwanthi De Chikera, depicts the physical and emotional cruelty meted out to the wife in the story. Ajith, the Asian husband, slaps Nanda, his wife, but she does not even attempt to ward him off. When he shouts at her, "Remember who you are—where you came from you low down slut. You will never be anything else to me," she does not retaliate in anger but says instead "Don't hit me" (5). In *The Bluest Eye*, Cholly's brutality towards Mrs. Breedlove is equally violent in its physicality: "Dropping to his knee, he struck her several times in the face" (33). In *Middle of Silence*, the man is a paraplegic, and since he is physically muted, the anger and abuse lie strongly in his words. In *The Bluest Eye*, the violence between Cholly and Mrs. Breedlove is very physical. This is just one small example of the violence that the students at AUW have either read about or experienced first-hand in their families and communities. Acid burns, rape, strangulation, bride burning, feticide, stalking are some of the increasingly manifested forms of violence in the homes and in the streets of Asia. Thus, it is never very difficult to make the students understand how and why violence is perpetrated in certain communities or towards other communities.

Conclusion

Teaching a text which is not 'your own' does have certain limitations. Personally, I was fearful lest the students at AUW have difficulty in understanding or recognizing the idioms of the West and of African American historicity. But to my great wonder, they were not only able to understand the multi-pronged nuances that the multi-cultural text raised, they were able to pull the issues out of the Western context and place them in an Asian one. It is greatly satisfying to see how the students captured the sentiments of discrimination, isolation, hierarchy, race, class, beauty, women, body and patriarchy.

Works Cited

Bhabha, Homi. *The Location of Culture*. London. Routledge. 1994. Print.

Bhuiya, A., Sharmin, T., Hanifi, S.M.A. (2003). "Nature of domestic violence against women in a rural area of Bangladesh: implication for preventive interventions." *Health, Population & Nutrition*, 21(1): 48–54. Retrieved from http://www.jhpn.net/index.php/jhpn/article/download/184/179.

Chikera, Ruwanthie De, *Middle of Silence*. Colombo. ICES. 2001. Print.

Cormier-Hamilton, Patrice. "Black Naturalism and Toni Morrison: The Journey Away from Self-love in *The Bluest Eye*." *MELUS*. 19.4 (Winter 1994): 109–127.Print.

'Delhi is unsafe for women as on December 16.' *Hindustan Times*. New Delhi, September 11, 2013.

Immigration and Refugee Board of Canada (2004). Bangladesh: Violence against women, especially domestic violence; state protection and resources available to survivors of abuse. *Immigration and Refugee Board of Canada*. BGD42249.E. Retrieved from

http://www.unhcr.org/refworld/docid/403dd1e40.html.

Leela Dube. "Caste and Women," in *Women's Studies in India: A Reader* ed. Mary E. John. New Delhi. Penguin. 2008. Print

Morrison, Toni. *The Bluest Eye*. New York. Random House. 1970.

Nadeau, Kathleen, and Sangita Rayamajhi. *Women's Roles in Asia*. Santa Barbara. Greenwood. 2013. Print.

National Institute for Population Research and Training (2007). *Bangladesh Demographic and Health Survey (BDHS)*. The Ministry of Health and Family Welfare. Retrieved from http://www.measuredhs.com/pubs/pdf/GF13/GF13.pdf.

Pereira, Malin Walther. "Periodizing Toni Morrison's Work from *The Bluest Eye* to *Jazz*:

The Importance of *Tar Baby*."*MELUS*. 22. 3 (Fall 1997): 71–81. Print.

Roy, Arundhati. *The God of Small Things*. Penguin Books. New Delhi. 1997. Print.

Said, Edward. *Orientalism: Western Conceptions of the Orient*. Harmondsworth. Penguin. 1991.

Tharu, Susie. "Tracing Savitri's Pedigree: Victorian racism and the Image of Women in Indo-Anglian Literature." *Recasting Women: Essays in Colonial History*. Ed. Kumkum Sangari and SudeshVaid. New Delhi. Zubaan. 1989. 254–268.

Bodies, Music, and Embodied Cognition in Toni Morrison's Fictional Works

Anna Iatsenko

When Toni Morrison was awarded the Nobel Prize for literature, Professor Sture Allén declared during the ceremony that: "In her depiction of the world of the black people, in life as in legend, Toni Morrison has given the Afro-American people their history back, piece by piece" (Allén). Indeed, Morrison's novels have always been deeply historical, but the history she is concerned with is not based on the tracing of dates or historical figures, but rather is that of experience. It is well known, for example, that Morrison's project in *Beloved* aims to fill in the gaps left by previous slave narratives, undertaking to present to readers the psychological and emotional experience of slavery. Morrison deploys this engagement with experience in her fiction, as Professor Allén says: "[Her] novels invite the reader to partake at many levels, and at varying degrees of complexity. Still, the most enduring impression they leave is of empathy, compassion with one's fellow human beings" (*Online*).

It is this engagement with experience that makes Morrison's fiction a privileged site for exploration of how literature can enrich our understanding of being in the world. This will be the point of departure of the present essay, in which I look at the strategies that Morrison deploys in her fiction in order to engage with the reader experientially. I will argue that what makes Morrison's writing so effective is her use of vocal and musical strategies within her language and narration. Furthermore, the presence of voice and music in Morrison's novels also enlightens us on the issues relating to how we think about being in the world: the characters she creates and the ways these characters evolve and relate to the worlds they inhabit are infused with music, leading me to question Merleau-Ponty's phenomenological outlook on experience as being silently physical and not also vocal and musical.

One of the most prominent features of Morrison's fictional works resides in the fact that she constructs narratives where experience of brutal environments which the characters inhabit, reveals devastating impacts on women and children. Starting from her very first novel—*The Bluest Eye*—which tells the story of Pecola Breedlove's descent into madness, Morrison exposes the fact that it is the world in which Pecola evolves that ultimately drives the character mad. Indeed, this moving narrative denounces the devastating impact of internalized racial hatred upon the young female protagonist, whom Morrison describes in the foreword to the 1999 Vintage edition of the novel as: "the most delicate member of society: a child; the most vulnerable member: a female" (Morrison, *Bluest* iii). However, there is another aspect to Morrison's novel: while denouncing the omnipresence of the racial legacy in African American communities, she also outlines the resilience, beauty and immense creativity that are apparent in the musicality of the language used.

In *The Bluest Eye*, attention to musical elements are often presented through the eyes of young Claudia who comments on her fascination with listening to the exchanges between the adult women: "It was autumn too when Mr. Henry came. Our roomer. Our roomer. The words ballooned from the lips and hovered about our heads—silent, separate and pleasantly mysterious. My mother was all ease and satisfaction in discussing his coming" (7). Interestingly, Claudia's fascination is not directed towards what the word "roomer" means, but how it is pronounced. The repetition of the double vowel "oo" in the words "roomer" and "ballooned" reinforces the accentuation of sound rather than the content of what is heard. Furthermore, the description of the presence of the sound as "balloon[ing] from the lips" and "hover[ing] about our heads" links the sound back to the body and creates an impression of the actual pronunciation of, and therefore embodiment, of sound. A few lines later in the text, Claudia comments:

> Frieda and I are washing Mason jars. We do not hear their words, but with grown-ups we listen to and watch out for their voices…
>
> Their conversation is like a gently wicked dance: sound meets sound, curtsies, shimmies, and retires. Another sound enters but is upstaged by still another: the two circle each other and stop. Sometimes their words move in lofty spirals; other times they take strident leaps, and all of it is punctuated with warm-pulsed laughter—like the throb of a heart made of jelly. The edge, the curl, the thrust of their emotions is always clear to

> Frieda and me. We do not, cannot, know the meanings of all their words,
> for we are nine and ten years old. So we watch their faces, their hands,
> their feet, and listen for truth in timbre. (9–10)

The simile used in the quotation above to describe the sound of the adults'
verbal exchange as a "gently wicked dance", rather than evoking dance in
some abstract sense, takes the discussion of language into the domain of the
physical by comparing it to the dancers' bodies and the actions dancers
perform via the use of the active verbs such as "meets," "shimmies,"
"curtsies," and "retires". This structuring of description with active verbs is
repeated throughout the passage, where active verbs clearly dominate the
syntactical structure of the sentences concerned with the function of verbal
exchange. Here, in a very precise manner, Claudia describes language not as
doing something in the semantic sense—because she is unconcerned with
the meanings of the words the adults are using—but she identifies the
importance of sound within language, which for her is primary to the
function of the linguistic sign. What Claudia encodes in her speech is not a
direct correspondence between the signifier and the signified; rather, she
creates new connections between words and her experience of their sounds.
In contrast to Saussure, who positions the voice as the vehicle for the
spoken sign and who associates sound with the signifier, Claudia clearly
demonstrates that it is the voice itself that is meaningful and so sound
becomes meaning in the child's relationship with and experience of the
surrounding world.

Where in *The Bluest Eye* Morrison sketches out some clues to the
importance of sound and voice with respect to the individual's relationship
to the world, in her subsequent fiction she takes this project a step further
and engages more explicitly with sound. With *Beloved* she creates a text
where the importance of sound and music is problematized on a number of
interesting levels both with respect to content and form of narration. From
its inception, the project of *Beloved* is vocally oriented as it attempts to fill
the gaps left by the unvoiced past of slavery. When writing about *Beloved*,
Jill Matus states that:

> Morrison's interviews from 1987–89, when *Beloved* was being written and
> published, attest to her own passionate reclamation of an unspeakable
> history. *Beloved* is born from her recognition that traditional slave
> narratives always 'drew a veil' over the shocking and painful incidents of
> their past, pleading that such things were too terrible to relate. (104)

Indeed, Matus is absolutely right and texts such as Harriet A. Jacobs's *Incidents in the Life of a Slave Girl* (1861) perfectly illustrate the silences that Morrison's project attempts to fill.[1] In *Beloved*, the importance of the voice becomes quite literal—Morrison identifies the silences with respect to the trauma of slavery and, simultaneously, acknowledges and acts upon the need to voice these silences in her writing in order to work through the trauma of slavery. Thus, *Beloved* is conceived as a project which allows Morrison to "act out and work through" issues that have been historically, narratively, and collectively disavowed.

Morrison tackles the problem of what she calls "national amnesia" by constructing a narrative, which permits the vocal expression of the experience of slavery. However, she does not do this indirectly, by telling her reader what slavery feels like in a remote, disengaged manner; rather, she tells a story that involves the reader in the experience itself. This involvement is created through Morrison's use of embodied cognition, which proposes that the ways we make meaning of the world is rooted within our physical body. In *Beloved*, a number of Morrison's narrative techniques foreground the importance of the body in experience: the main healer of the narrative—Baby Suggs—heals the community by connecting people to their bodies rather than religious faith; Sethe's memory-triggers are primarily physical rather than mental operations and these set in motion the flashbacks that structure the narrative; the effectiveness of Beloved as a character is due to the fact that she is an embodied ghost whose presence is graphically physical throughout most of the novel. However, for Morrison, it is not simply the flesh that apprehends the outside world—her conceptualization of embodied cognition positions the body as speaking and singing and it is these voices that must be taken into consideration.

One of the most striking and clear examples in *Beloved* is the role of Baby Suggs and, in particular, her preaching in the clearing. This scene is set

---

[1] When telling of her enslavement and escape from slavery, Harriet never puts into words the feelings she associates with the experiences she describes. Her narrative is full of detailed descriptions of actions, or pain inflicted on her, but she does not comment on any of the psychological aspects of her life nor does she tell the reader her own feelings. One particularly striking example of such absence in the narrative is located in the chapter entitled "A Loophole of Retreat" where Jacobs describes being confined in a garret—a space nine feet long and seven feet wide with three inches at the highest point between the floor and the roof. Able to crawl around this space only occasionally, Jacobs spends a few years in this space suffering frostbite in winter and strenuous heat in the summer, listening to the voices of her own children without being able to communicate with them. While she mentions a few words about her physical condition, she never says anything concerning the emotional pain that the situation inflicted upon her.

in an extremely noisy atmosphere where children, women and men create a joyous cacophony at the preacher's command. This scene is immediately followed by a moment of silence in which Baby Suggs explains the importance of their bodies in connection to happiness: "She told them that the only grace they could have was the grace they could imagine. That if they could not see it, they would not have it" (103). This surprising sentence reported by the narrator with rather abstract and religious overtones is then rendered very concrete in direct speech quoting Baby Suggs' own words:

> "Here," she said, "in this here place, we flesh; flesh that weeps, laughs; flesh that dances on bare feet in grass. Love it. Love it hard. Yonder they do not love your flesh. They despise it. [...] No more do they love the skin on your back. Yonder they flay it. And O my people they do not love your hands. Those they only use, tie, bind, chop off and leave empty. Love your hands! Love them. Raise them up and kiss them. Touch others with them, pat them together, stroke them on your face 'cause they don't love that either. *You* got to love it, *you*! [...] This is flesh I'm talking about here. Flesh that needs to be loved. Feet that need to rest and to dance; backs that need support; shoulders that need arms, strong arms I'm telling you... The dark, dark liver – love it, love it, and the beat and beating heart, love that too. More than eyes or feet. More than lungs that have yet to draw free air. More than your life-holding womb and your life-giving private parts, hear me now, love your heart. For this is the prize." Saying no more, she stood up then and danced with her twisted hip the rest of what her heart had to say while the others opened their mouths and gave her the music. Long notes held until the four-part harmony was perfect enough for their deeply loved flesh. (emphasis in the original, 103–4)

After the deep silence in the clearing, Baby Suggs uses the power of her rhetorical language to assemble the bodies fragmented by the experience of slavery. Her use of the words "here" and "yonder" create a space physically, but also semantically where the assembling becomes possible. However, it is the reported dancing and singing that validate the words uttered by Baby Suggs: she dances to confirm her words and those present sing along with her to confirm their understanding of her words. In this particular instance, the voices come together to identify and validate the content of what was said and literally to embody the words of freedom uttered by the healer.

For the character of Beloved, the voice is also important and she is constructed in a way that makes her physical presence undeniably vocal. The narrator comments on the first words she speaks as follows: "... her voice was so low and rough each one looked at the other two. They heard the voice first later the name" (62). Here, as in *The Bluest Eye*, the voice clearly precedes the semantic content of what is being said. Furthermore, when Sethe finally makes the link between Beloved and her own dead daughter, the moment of realization is framed by Beloved's voice singing the song Sethe had made up for her children:

> When the click came Sethe didn't know what it was. Afterward it was clear as daylight that the click came at the very beginning—a beat, almost, before it started; before she heard three notes; before the melody was even clear. Leaning forward a little, Beloved was humming softly.
>
> It was then, when Beloved finished humming that Sethe recalled the click – the settling of pieces into place designed and made especially for them. [...] She simply turned her head and looked at Beloved's profile: the chin, mouth, nose, forehead, copied and exaggerated in the huge shadow the fire threw on the wall behind her. [...]
>
> The click had clicked; things were where they ought to be or poised and ready to glide in.
>
> "I made that song up," said Sethe. "I made it up and sang it to my children. Nobody knows that song but me and my children."
>
> Beloved turned to look at Sethe. "I know it," she said. (206–7)

Here, on a very literal level, Beloved's singing acts as a memory trigger for Sethe. Moreover, the way that the narrator comments on Sethe's experience of the singing suggests that something happens already "a beat, almost, before it started" (207). However, rather than account for this "click" in terms of time, the narrator embeds this elusive moment further into the singing "before she heard three notes; before the melody was even finished" (207). Here, the time markers "before" appear in relation to music. This slippage between the moment that precedes the singing and the moment when the melody finishes is expressed in terms of the act of singing and not time *per se*, pointing to the fact that it is the song itself that leads Sethe to feel the "click". Only later is Sethe able to contextualize the experience in terms of the song that she sang to her children. In the moment when "the click" clicked she is fully, experientially, in the music and this allows her to recognize her dead child now embodied in Beloved.

Other extremely powerful moments are present in *Beloved* when music-making voices come to the fore. My examples illustrate the workings of the voices and music in terms of content, but there is one particular aspect of the novel that exposes how music also works formally on the narrative level.

This example is located in the second section of the novel, in the section that closes the monologues performed by Sethe, Denver and Beloved. Interestingly, the scene is at first presented from the perspective of Stamp Paid who hears the voices coming from inside 124 Bluestone Road:

> What he heard, as he moved toward the porch, he didn't understand. Out on Bluestone Road he thought he heard a conflagration of hasty voices—loud, urgent, all speaking at once so he could not make out what they were talking about or to whom [...] something was wrong with the order of the words and he couldn't describe or cipher it to save his life. All he could make out was the word *mine*. The rest of it stayed outside his minds reach [...] When he got to the steps, the voices drained suddenly to less than a whisper [...] They had become an occasional mutter—like the interior sounds a woman makes when she believes she is alone and unobserved in her work: a *sth* when she misses the needle's eye; a soft moan when she sees another chip in her one good platter; the low friendly argument with which she greets the hens. (emphasis in the original, 202–3)

Through this focalization, the narrator suggests that Stamp Paid is looking to explain the voices he hears in terms of his own experience. The narrator makes a point of mentioning that Stamp Paid was unable to "cipher" the voices, giving a clue to his epistemological approach to what he hears. Indeed, the narrator contextualizes Stamp Paid's understanding of what he is experiencing as something that is familiar to him – the role of women's voices of in their everyday chores. But when the text presents us with the actual words that are uttered by the women of 124, the reader quickly understands the extent to which Stamp Paid misreads the voices. When the text switches perspective from the outside to the inside of the house, the reader is confronted with the three monologues of Sethe, Denver and Beloved respectively. The monologues, presented in a style that is narratologically close to stream of consciousness technique, make explicit what the reader has only been guessing up until now—that the women's deep personal traumas are finally verbalized. As we read through the monologues and arrive at Beloved's words, the lines of print begin to drift apart. Indeed, Beloved's monologue is clearly marked visually by the presence of spaces between phrases and the absence of punctuation and capitalizations which create a very demanding reading experience: the reader is constantly solicited by the gaps in the text to create continuity or, on the contrary, to separate the units of meaning.

The fourth section, following the three monologues, also begins stylistically like the monologues, but quickly turns into something very different. Beginning in prose, the opening of this section seems to take up Beloved's monologue again where she, in the first person, loosely fills in the semantic gaps that were present in the previous monologue. This rather long paragraph is then followed by a visibly identifiable break and the narrative form collapses altogether into what looks like poetry. Indeed, the lines of text that follow are disjointed, with one or two phrases occupying a line. However, rather than considering this form as strictly poetic, I would like to suggest that, in fact, Morrison chooses the song as the governing formal principle for this section. In an interview with Marsha Darling, Morrison identifies this passage as "a kind of threnody" (249).[2] A threnody is a lament and, etymologically, the term refers to a "wailing" "song" (*Concise OED*, 1493). Moreover, my reason for reading this section of the text as a song is twofold: first, in order to make sense of the words on the page, the reader needs to identify the voices and, secondly, the repetition of personal pronouns "I" and "you" clearly marks a chorus where the voices merge to become completely indistinguishable at the very end of the section:

> I drank your blood
> I brought you milk
> You forgot to smile
> I loved you
> You hurt me
> You came back to me
> You left me
>
> I waited for you
> You are mine
> You are mine
> You are mine (255)

Here, the form of the text and the grief expressed by the words of the women collaborate to create an account of a very personal, intimate experience of the enslaved past. The loss of a parent, of a child, of a sibling is conveyed to the reader in a very particular form of engagement. The fact that the text collapses from prose into verse attests to the fact that the

---

[2] In Taylor-Guthrie 246-54.

content is indeed "unspeakable", but by shifting from prose into song the text sings the "unspeakable."[3]

It is clear that Morrison's engagement with experience permeates her works. After *Beloved*, in *Jazz*, she further elaborates the technique of using music to create a narrative in which form stands equal to meaning. Rather than telling what the jazz age is about, she constructs a narration which embodies the music of the period.[4] In subsequent novels such as *Love*, *A Mercy*, and *Home*, Morrison also explores experience in a similar manner. Indeed, the mastery of language and storytelling that Morrison displays is always geared towards unveiling, uncovering, exposing some part of experiential knowledge that has either been explicitly forgotten or taken for granted. However, Morrison's fiction greatly exceeds the scope of the fictional world, because her fiction also has the capacity to teach us something about experience outside the diegetic level of narration. By transcending fictional ontologies, Morrison's fiction becomes a workshop for experimentation with our relationship to knowledge where she constantly questions the process by which we engage with, perceive and create the world that surrounds us. Such questions have also puzzled phenomenologists who conclude that the body is our primary source of contact with the world. In his seminal work *Phenomenology of Perception*, Maurice Merleau-Ponty clearly states that the body is the primary locus of our experience of and in the world:

> In so far as, when I reflect on the essence of subjectivity, I find it bound up with that of the body and that of the world, this is because my existence as subjectivity is merely one with my existence as a body and with the existence of the world, and because the subject that I am, when taken concretely, is inseparable from this body and this world. The ontological world and body which we find at the core of the subject are not the world or body as idea, but on the one hand the world itself contracted into a comprehensive grasp, and on the other the body itself as a knowing-body. (475)

Whereas for Merleau-Ponty cognition is embodied, it is also silent—he does not acknowledge the domain of the spoken in the experiential relationship to the world. Rather, sound is secondary for him and part of a system which

---

[3] For other discussions of musical elements in *Beloved* please consult: Rodrigues "The Telling of *Beloved*." 153-69; Kitts 495-523; Reed 55-71; Eckstein 271-83.
[4] For a thorough analysis of the technical musical elements of jazz music used in *Jazz* please consult the following: Rodriguez "Experiencing *Jazz*." 447-454; Rice 153-180.

serves only to describe the world, and his interest lies mainly in the "unspoken *cogito*" (468).[5] Morrison's fiction, however, demonstrates that embodied cognition relies heavily on sound and musicality. As the narrator of *Beloved* states when commenting on the women's singing during the exorcism of Beloved: "In the beginning there were no words. In the beginning was the sound, and they all knew what that sound sounded like" (305).

Indeed, Morrison's fictional works display thorough engagement with elements of voice and music. These elements are present both on the level of form and content and they collaborate to engage readers aurally with the texts. It is thanks to this engagement that Morrison is able to communicate experientially through her texts: rather than telling her readers what it is "like" to experience life from her characters' perspectives, she creates narratives which make the readers engage with these experiences directly. Thus, her texts become sites of embodied knowledge where the aural holds a privileged position. More globally, however, through her mastery of the aural Morrison re-establishes the importance of the voice and musical perception in the relationship to the world, suggesting that our knowledge and experience are also acquired through a deep relationship to sound, voice and music.

Works Cited

Allén, Sture. "Award Ceremony Speech." *Nobel Lectures, Literature.* Nobel Media AB 2013. Web. 10 Sept. 2013. ‹http://www.nobelprize.org.nobel_prize/literature/laureates/1993/presentation-speech.html›

Darling, Marsha. "In the Realm of Responsibility: A Conversation with Toni Morrison" Taylor-Guthrie 246–54.

Eckstein, Lars. "A Love Supreme: Jazzthetic Strategies in Toni Morrison's *Beloved*." *African American Review* 40:2 (2006): 271–283. Web. 28 Jan. 2011. ‹http://muse.jhu.edu›.

Jacobs, Harriet A. *Incidents in the Life of a Slave Girl. Written by Herself.* Boston: Published for the Author, 1861. *Documenting the American South.* 2003. University Library, University of North Carolina at Chapel Hill. Web. 10 Sept. 2013 ‹http://docsouth.unc.edu/fpn/jacobs/jacobs.html›

[5] For a more detailed discussion of Merleau-Ponty's problematic use of "unspoken *cogito*" see Shusterman 49-76.

Kitts, Lenore. "Toni Morrison and 'Sis Joe': The Musical Heritage of Paul D." *MSF Modern Fiction Studies* 52:2 (2006): 495–523. Web. 28 Jan 2011 ‹http://muse.jhu.edu›

Matus, Jill. *Toni Morrison*. Manchester: Manchester UP, 1998. Print.

Merleau-Ponty, Maurice. *Phenomenology of Perception*. Transl. Colin Smith. London: Routledge, 2002. Print.

Morrison, Toni. *A Mercy*. London: Vintage, 2009. Print.

—. *Beloved*. London: Vintage, 2005. Print.

—. *Home*. New York, Toronto: Knopf, 2012. Print.

—. *Jazz*. London: Vintage, 2005. Print.

—. *Love*. London: Vintage, 2004. Print.

—. *The Bluest Eye*. London: Vintage, 1999. Print.

Peach, Linden, ed. New Casebooks: Toni Morrison. New York: St. Martin's Press, 1998. Print.

Reed. Roxanne R. "The Restorative Power of Sound: A Case for Communal Catharsis in Toni Morrison's *Beloved*." *Journal of Feminist Studies in Religion* 23:1 (2007): 55–71. Web. 28 Jan. 2011. ‹http://muse.jhu.edu›.

Rice, Alan J. "'It Don't Mean a Thing If It Ain't Got That Swing': Jazz's Many Uses for Toni Morrison." Saadi A Simawe 153–180.

Rodrigues, Eusebio L. "Experiencing *Jazz*." *New Casebooks: Toni Morrison*. Linden Peach 447–454.

—. "The Telling of *Beloved*." *Journal of Narrative Technique*, 21:2 (1991): 153–169. Web. 03 Dec. 2012 ‹http://www.jstor.org/stable/30225328›.

Shusterman, Richard. *Body Consciousness: A Philosophy of Mindfulness and Somaesthetics*. Cambridge, Cambridge UP, 2008. Print

Simawe, Saadi A, ed. *Black Orpheus: Music In African American Fiction From the Harlem Renaissance to Toni Morrison*. New York: Garland, 2000. Print.

Taylor-Guthrie, Danielle, ed. *Conversations with Toni Morrison*. Jackson: University of Mississippi Press, 1994. Print.

"You your best thing, Sethe. You are": African American Maternal Experience in Toni Morrison's *Beloved*

Giulia Grillo Mikrut

The complexity of *Beloved* lies in the problem of "reading silence" (McDermott 75). Historically, silence was one of the primary conditions of the Black self. Through connection with the past and the Other, Morrison writes new subjects developing from a process of self-actualisation made possible thanks to a rejection of silence and an emphasis on vocalization. The journey towards agency and speech is achieved in various steps. Fragmentation is the starting point towards self-recovery and wholeness, as if it were the very first step to recovery.

Regarding African American women's history and narrative structure, Toni Morrison says that she thought of her novel *Sula* as a "cracked mirror, fragments and pieces we have to see independently and put together" (quoted in Taylor-Guthrie 127). Ron David argues that in *Beloved*, instead, "everything connects, everything fits—each of the parts contributes to the whole" (134). The structure of the novel is persistently convincing because of the "chain of causality" (David 134) with which Morrison tells the events represented in the novel, giving more focus to the "people instead of on the writing" (David 135). Angeletta Gourdine observes that in *Beloved*, "the voices of the novel tell their own story, but their story goes beyond the pages that contain it" (16). Morrison's words need to be read and interpreted several times in order to offer full understanding. As Cynthia Dobbs argues, "[Morrison's] prose, 'never giving you the whole story,' insists on the inability of *any* vocabulary to contain certain experiences. There are always gaps, excesses, slippages, shifting signs, sounds that we can't fully hear" (568). Altogether, these make the structure of the novel very sophisticated and complex. Every time we reread the novel, a new inter-

67

pretation becomes possible. If Zora Neale Hurston allows her characters to acquire a voice by depicting the journey of these voices from inaudibility to expression, Morrison employs a different construction: self-consciousness and speech are passed from one character to another. The characters' voices are never overwhelming, as if "there were no author, no ego, no anything between the people in the book and us" (David 133). It is perhaps this coordination that makes the novel so majestic. In *Beloved,* the narratorial voice shifts from omniscient to interior monologue (Pérez-Torres 179). This is to witness the formation and development of the characters' individual voices.

Parallel to the existence of a voice is the issue of identity. Henry Louis Gates, Jr. argues that Black writers "use a language in which blackness signifies absence," and, at the same time, he wonders how this Blackness can become a "source of identity" (quoted in N. Peterson 92). We therefore understand the implications arising from this matter. How can lack of something become source? In this case, Black writers generate personal identity from absence. Pérez-Torres detects that this deficiency is already tangible at the beginning of the story, where the text describes the house on 124 Bluestone: "124 WAS SPITEFUL" (Morrison, *Beloved* 3). Baby Suggs, is dead, Howard and Buglar, the sons, gone. Sethe lives in the house with her daughter, Denver, and a ghost. The reader is given a sense of the impossibility of referring to the past or even the future, as if both are absent: "The interplay between presence and absence, accepting and rejecting, appearing and disappearing, repeats and resurfaces throughout the course of *Beloved*" (Pérez-Torres 181).

The present becomes the real time frame in the novel. Pérez-Torres calls it the "static fictional present" (181), and it is deployed to argue the nonexistence of beingness of the past and, simultaneously, of the future. The future becomes possible only if the characters reveal how "the 'other' serves as an instrument in the construction of the self" (Moglen 17). In *Beloved,* temporality and identity equally contribute to the formation of self, which has moved from fragmentation to wholeness in a process that has enriched it with speaking agency.

The achievement of female speaking agency and self-realization in the maternal context involves relationships and love. Letting the characters interact and engage with each other offers a vivid illustration of their lives. The text's engagement with these two topics provides us with a rich set of symbols through which to understand the novel. Morrison's novel is so symbolically rich that it is open to a variety of interpretations that can nevertheless be held simultaneously. This unity from fragmentation, or wholeness out of diversity is another of the ways in which the novel's structure performs my argument about the move from fragmentation to wholeness. For instance, at the beginning of part two, the same sentence appears four times in two pages: "but nobody saw them falling" (Morrison, *Beloved* 205–06). Sethe's strength always allows her to stand up time and time again and to survive. When Beloved comes back into her life, she secludes herself and Denver within the walls of 124 Bluestone Road. This is why, when the three women—Sethe, Denver, and Beloved—are out on the ice skating, the "sky above them was another country" (205). Nobody can see them skating, nor falling. It may mean that, metaphorically, there is no "other" wanting to see them, as during the Middle Passage and slavery (and still today), when many white people did not want to acknowledge what was happening to African Americans, although they witnessed the atrocities committed against them.

Sethe's character is a problematic one. She suffers from guilt to a point that her whole environment and reality become surreal. For an extended time, this state of mind brings her to an incongruous account of the meaning of life. In this dream-resembling circumstance, when Beloved begins to hum Sethe's song, "the click came" (206). At this point, the reader needs to take a step away from the story to comprehend what is happening. The text brilliantly depicts the characters' psychological wellbeing and Sethe's process of self-actualization. Though we haven't got to self-actualization yet, this click leads to Sethe's equally problematic absorption by her child, which is part of her ongoing failure to recognize her self as whole and worthy of love.

Maternal Bonds

Morrison writes the novel with the aim of conveying a way to express some of the sorrow brought by slavery and its repercussions on African American women's (and maternal) bodies. Slavery is the clearest example of African Americans' objectification. In this regard, Ryan McDermott writes about Sethe's "divided flesh," suggesting that Sethe's divided body metaphorically reproduces "the structural divisions of slavery, which separates man from beast and robs the Black female slave of subjectivity while imposing upon her a distinctly biological expression of otherness" (81). Morrison writes, therefore, about what many other authors prefer instead to forget and ignore, and creates a marvelous concept in the form of a ghost girl. Accordingly, there are speculations about Beloved's identity. Martha J. Cutter asks the same question–who Beloved really is–and forms her own interpretation of the two passages where Beloved talks about the one white man she knew and also answers Paul D by closing her eyes and letting him know that "[i]n the dark my name is Beloved" (Morrison, *Beloved* 88). Cutter connects the two arguments to the dialogue between Stamp Paid and Paul D, where the former recounts the story of "a girl locked up in the house with a Whiteman over by Deer Creek. Found him dead last summer and the girl gone. Maybe that's her. Folks say he had her in there since she was a pup" (277). In Cutter's view, the girl in the latter example is possibly the same girl calling herself Beloved at 124 Bluestone (Morrison, *Beloved* 88). Again, this is one more possible interpretation.

Whatever place Beloved came from, I believe that Morrison's intention is to let us observe the characters' responses when in the presence of the ghost. With Sethe, for instance, the text depicts a sense of wholeness at the end of the story while from the beginning of the novel we first notice how she sacrifices her own child to prevent her from experiencing similar atrocities to those inflicted on Sethe by Schoolteacher. Sethe "commits self-murder; she kills a part of herself by killing her child" (Koolish 185). With time, Sethe becomes emotionally stronger, and when Edward Bodwin enters the property at 124 Bluestone Road and Sethe mistakes him for Schoolteacher, she acts instinctively, knowing that she needs to keep her family safe:

> Sethe feels her eyes burn and it may have been to keep them clear that she looks up. They sky is blue and clear. Not one touch of death in the definite green of the leaves. It is when she lowers her eyes to look again at the loving faces before her that she sees him. Guiding the mare, slowing down, his black hat wide-brimmed enough to hide his face but not his purpose. He is coming into her yard and he is coming for her best thing. She hears wings. Little hummingbirds stick needle beaks right through her headcloth into her hair and beat their wings. And if she thinks anything it is no. No no. Nonono. She flies. The ice pick is not in her hand, it is her hand. (308–09)

Her option is no longer to kill herself due to the murder of her own child. She is instead ready to attack the white man—the oppressor—"claiming for herself a kind of wholeness by attacking, instead of a part of her self, a white man, emblem of the original threat" (Koolish 185). Regarding the passage above, Kimberly Chabot Davis writes:

one way to free oneself from the horrors of the past is to reenact and reconfigure the past in the present, as Sethe does with an ice pick at the end of the novel, attacking not her own children this time but the white man Bodwin, whom she perceives as a reincarnation of her slave master Schoolteacher. (251)

At first, we read the Bodwins as a family against slavery and segregation. However, at the end of the novel they are depicted differently; they are not the abolitionists we thought they were originally. At the same time, this explains that they are not exempt from racism and the belief that Black people are subservient to whites either. After hearing Nelson Lord telling her to take care of herself, Denver decides to find a job and therefore visits Mr. and Mrs. Bodwin (Morrison, *Beloved* 297). When she is about to exit their home after having spoken to the maid, Janey Wagon, a statuette catches Denver's eye:

> With those assurances, Denver left, but not before she had seen, sitting on a shelf by the back door, a blackboy's mouth full of money. His head was thrown back farther than a head could go, his hands were shoved in his pockets. Bulging like moons, two eyes were all the face he had above the gaping red mouth. His hair was a cluster of raised, widely spaced dots made of nail heads. And he was on his knees. His mouth, wide as a cup, held the coins needed to pay for a delivery or some other small service, but could just as well have held buttons, pins or crab-apple jelly. Painted across the pedestal he knelt on were the words "At Yo Service." (300)

This figurine might represent a Black boy with a possibly lynched head and his nail heads might represent African American hair. The passage above cannot be used to prove that the Bodwins are Abolitionists or not. What the passage expresses is racism in the culture of the community. Although this statue is a reminder of slavery, Denver is certain that the Bodwins are good people. Janey Wagon tells her, "[t]hey used to be good whitefolks," to which Denver answers, "[o]h, yeah. They good. Can't say they ain't good. I wouldn't trade them for another pair, tell you that" (300).

Although Sethe does not know about the statuette, when Edward Bodwin rides on his cart to her residence at 124 Bluestone Road, Sethe has the "chance to play out the scene with a completely different outcome" (Koolish 186). By letting her defeat a white man, Sethe is offered the opportunity, and terms, to think about her own situation—saving her family from the white oppressor— and metaphorically to take revenge on behalf of all the African American people, the "sixty million and more" (Morrison, *Beloved*, Dedication Page) who died during the Middle Passage. Thus, the author returns the power of agency to Sethe, who can overcome her painful past. Not to be forgotten is that the ice pick passage is an enactment of extreme violence and it is Ella who brings wisdom to the situation stressing that violence is not the answer, not even against the white man.

In *Beloved*, Morrison attempts to recreate, or, as Setefanus Suprajitno writes, "reconstruct her women to be women, and not just mothers and daughters" (64). Sethe becomes a woman by addressing and 'rememorying' her difficult maternal history. In *Beloved*, vocalization becomes the way through which women give a voice to their bodies, they finally embrace the act of speech, and become active subject in the society. This is how the African American female characters in novel learn how "to talk back" in an attempt to express their transition from object to subject: "the liberated voice" (hooks, *Talking* 9).

The Maternal Body

As Morrison has explained, the starting point of *Beloved* is the necessity to keep in touch with ancestors. In the foreword to James Van Der Zee, Owen Dodson, and Camille Billops' book, Morrison states that "[t]he ancestor lives as long as there are those who remember" (quoted in Van Der Zee, Dodson and Billops, "Foreword"). The novel is the result of a memory reconstruction process. Morrison often talks about "national amnesia" (quoted in Taylor-Guthrie 257) when discussing the effects and repercussions of slavery as something that neither Blacks nor whites want to remember. Therefore, to overcome this amnesia, Morrison wrote a novel where a female slave, Sethe, articulates her pain about the institution of slavery in relation to her role as mother. The act of remembering to achieve healing is painful. Morrison underlines this in the novel when Amy Denver, a white woman who helps Sethe deliver her fourth child on the banks of the Ohio River, tells her, "[a]nything dead coming back to life hurts" (Morrison, *Beloved* 42). The vision of her children helps Sethe overcome the pain inflicted on her body by schoolteacher and his nephews. Motherhood is most important to Sethe, who is indisputably convinced that her children are her "best thing" (321). *Beloved* thus "explores maternity, not from a male point of view or as a cultural projection, but as an interface between life and death *from within a mother*" (Demetrakopoulos 53). Terry Caesar explains that in *Beloved*, the concepts of motherhood and of being an enslaved woman "profoundly contaminate" each other and so become "virtually inseparable" (113).

When Paul D returns to Sethe's life, she is a free woman, although isolated in the house on 124 Bluestone Road and entrapped in the painful memories of her past, which she tries to keep at bay as much as she can. Sethe's first feeling of freedom is described when she reaches Baby Suggs in Ohio and lives there with her children and Baby Suggs for twenty-eight days. Although it is rather arduous, during these four weeks, Sethe is able to claim herself for the very first time. She thinks, "[f]reeing yourself was one thing; claiming ownership of that freed self was another" (Morrison, *Beloved* 111–12). By crossing the Ohio River, Sethe crossed the borders between slavery and freedom, life and death, present and past, as well as "being and non-being" (Gourdine 22).

The ambivalence of "being and not being," of remembering and forgetting as well as of burying and reviving is rather problematic in this novel. To speak the "unspeakable thoughts, unspoken" (Morrison, *Beloved* 235) becomes a way in which the novel revives the buried. To forget and to remember is one of the book's complex themes. Rushdy comments, "[t]his tension between needing to bury the past as well as needing to revive it, between a necessary remembering and an equally necessary forgetting, exists in both the author and her narrative" (569). When discussing the significance of forgetting in *Beloved*, Susan Bowers refers to the term "eschaton" (Bowers, *Beloved* 60), which Douglas Robinson explains as "that which stands between the familiar and whatever lies beyond" (xii–xiii). Comparing the "eschaton" to a veil, Bowers argues that the "eschaton" in *Beloved* is forgetting (60).

Morrison often explains her duty to write "from a double perspective of accusation and hope, of criticizing the past and caring for the future" (qtd. in Rushdy 575). In *Beloved*, her aim is to tell "a story not to pass on" (Morrison, *Beloved* 323) and initiate a process of historical recovery. The novel enables the characters to retell a story from the perspective of "African Americans as subjects rather than as objects" (Pal 2441), giving them agency. To do so, African Americans must be cleaned of the metaphoric dirt that white people have placed on their bodies, "dirtying them so badly they couldn't like themselves anymore. Dirtying them so bad they forgot who they were and couldn't think it up" (paraphrasing Morrison, *Beloved* 295). Dirt, in this sense, can be interpreted as the horrific experiences to which African Americans were subject during the Middle Passage and slavery. Bowers therefore wonders how it is possible to transform dirtiness into knowledge, and also how to give voice back to Black women:

> The struggle of *Beloved*'s characters to confront the effects of the brutality and to recover their human dignity, their selves "dirtied" by White oppression—to transform their experiences into knowledge—is presented in the form of a slave narrative that can be read as a model for contemporary readers attempting to engage these brutal realities. (Bowers 62)

Fear of dirtiness is something that many characters in the novel experience. The institution of slavery "dirtied" Sethe, Denver, Paul D, Baby Suggs, Ella, and Stamp Paid in a way that becomes impossible for them to forget. However, as Bowers argues, "[r]emembering is part of reversing the 'dirtying' that robbed slaves of self-esteem" (63) and it is precisely what the text allows the characters to do. By claiming the need to remember in order to forget, the characters enact a process of self-healing. In Sethe, maternal bonds help her character enact this self-healing process. Her love for her children—maternal love—is "too thick" (Morrison, *Beloved* 193). Firstly, it helps her deny the necessity of remembering the past; then it changes her life and makes her feel the need to initiate the recovery process. In this novel, the process of claiming the female self fortifies the power of motherhood.

Morrison focuses on three women in *Beloved*: Sethe, a mother, and Beloved and Denver, her two daughters. The author uses feminine traits to depict events that occur in the text: sisterhood and daughterhood (Denver and Beloved), pregnancy, the menstrual cycle, and childbirth (Sethe) are segments that can be symbolically identified. As an example, when Sethe sees Beloved for the first time, her "bladder filled to capacity" (61), which could be seen as a woman's waters breaking. Together, these segments are deployed to argue for the significance of slavery and its legacy for Black female bodies. According to Stephanie Demetrakopoulos, "the institution of slavery, the atrocity of historical time, denies Sethe her mothering and destroys the natural cycles of maternal bonding" (52). Slavery strips Baby Suggs, Sethe's mother-in-law, of her eight children: "I had eight. Every one of them gone away from me. Four taken, four chased ... Eight children and that's all I remember" (Morrison, *Beloved* 6). Although slavery deprives both men and women of their rights, women are doubly plagued: they are oppressed due to their gender and deprived of their nurturing capacity, as in the case of Baby Suggs. The problem of subjectivity and maternal capacity deprivation are now clear to be central issues in Morrison's novel.

Furthermore, *Beloved* tells the story of Sethe, a slave on a plantation in Kentucky called Sweet Home. We notice the irony, since the plantation is never a "sweet" place for the slaves, although, before schoolteacher's arrival, the white master, Mr Garner, treats slaves in a more humane way. The name of the plantation recalls the expression "home sweet home." At Sweet Home, slaves are treated fairly well until Mr Garner dies. His successor is schoolteacher, Mr Garner's brother-in-law. Schoolteacher enacts dehumanizing projects on Black male and female slaves. He studies their "characteristics"—behaving as an amateur scientist—categorizing them as if they were animals. Sethe and the other slaves are brutally treated and abused, so Sethe decides to escape. Sethe reaches her children and Baby Suggs in Lorraine, Ohio, and is only able to enjoy twenty-eight days of freedom before Schoolteacher and the slave catchers find her. At that moment, murder corresponds to an instinctive act. She does not apply reason to it. She just acts.

The woodshed where the murder is committed can be interpreted as slavery's "central trauma" (Bast 1076). The act gives Sethe equivocal agency to claim ownership of her children—a love "too thick" (193)—although she cannot at first verbalise her experience in the woodshed. Wyatt writes that Sethe "finds speech blocked … A gap remains at the heart of the story, which the omniscient narrator subsequently fills in" (476). At the same time, this act produces divergent responses in the community and the reader. When reading this specific passage in the novel, I could not avoid recalling a statement by Amram to Caleb, two characters in *Moses, Man of the Mountain*, a novel by Zora Neale Hurston. Amram tells Caleb, "[y]ou are up against a hard game when you got to die to beat it" (6). I think these words can be useful in the process of understanding the murder Sethe commits, since they evoke both a sense of complete powerlessness—you need to die to beat the system—and, at the same time, of agency, since to die is a way to become an active subject. These kinds of feelings were widely spread among slaves.

When interviewed by Gloria Naylor, Morrison offered her own perspective on the act:

> A woman loved something other than herself so much. She had placed all of the value of her life in something outside herself. That the woman who killed her children loved her children so much; they were the best part of her and she would not see them sullied. She would not see them hurt. (Naylor 207)

Sethe sees her children as her "best thing" (Morrison, *Beloved* 321). By "nourishing them, she nourishes herself" (Moglen 29). She transfers her own ego to an external individual, and she will not accept that her own "best things" must submit to the power of schoolteacher. This interpretation allows the reader to understand (at least partly) the murder. Sethe does not know any better; nobody ever taught her any better. Brought up without a mother, Sethe acts out her own concept of motherhood. At that time, in that place, Sethe acts emotionally and thinks that to take away the life of her "best things" is a better option than to allow Schoolteacher to take them all back to Sweet Home.

Sethe's love is "too thick" (193). In my opinion, it is possible to argue that Sethe's ego is originally transferred to her children. The final return of the ego to the body coincides with the novel's end. This movement, however, demonstrates that Sethe has forgotten about her own self. It is only when Paul D eventually comes back to 124 Bluestone Road, telling her, "[y]ou your best thing, Sethe. You are" (322) that the circumstances change. Doubting Paul D's words, Sethe answers, "Me? Me?" (322). Lost and confused, Sethe finally comprehends Paul D's words, realizing that her own strength, not her children's, has guided her all through life: it helped her to claim herself already once earlier when she reached Ohio and lived as a free woman for twenty-eight days before schoolteacher's arrival. Conversely, after having committed infanticide, Sethe becomes lost again. In this complex novel, her act of qualified, and compromised, love—to kill her child so as not to let schoolteacher claim ownership—is, from my perspective, the real starting point of Sethe's self-actualization. The level of love Sethe feels for her own children progressively becomes the principal constituent of her identity fragmentation. Morrison explained this in an interview with Gloria Naylor: "The best thing that is in us is also the thing that makes us sabotage ourselves" (qtd. in Lavon 29). Sethe's love—"the best thing in us"—makes her sabotage her own existence simply because she will not permit outside elements to conspire against her best things: her children.

The tragic act that Sethe commits helps us ponder slavery's dramatic effects. A daughter deprived of her mother, and simultaneously a mother who would rather see her own children dead rather than having them live under the institution of slavery—or, as Demetrakopoulos puts it, "rather than allow their souls to be devoured by slavery" (52)—becomes a good example of "paradoxical polarities in motherhood" (53). The act turns Sethe both into a criminal and a victim.

Sethe is not only a mother, but a daughter as well. Her mother nurses her for just two weeks, and after that, she is sent back to work in the plantations; at that point, Nan an African American nursemaid begins to take care of Sethe. When Sethe's mother is later hanged, Nan continues to take care of her. In the novel, Sethe explains her own wish to have been able to be a daughter. She says, "like a daughter, which is what I wanted to be and would have been if my ma'am had been able to get out of the rice long enough before they hanged her and let me be one" (240). The novel turns from an historical novel, it tells the real story of many African American slaves, to a novel about Sethe's womanhood and her concept of maternal bonds. As part of this journey, it is possible to identify a movement from internal fragmentation to wholeness and freedom through the activation of an internal healing process within the female Black subjects in *Beloved*.

Elizabeth Fox-Genovese argues that Sethe's act of infanticide possibly is a "desperate act of self-definition," since, "by claiming her child absolutely, she claims her identity as a mother, not a breeder" (112). The terrible act of killing her own daughter "forces Sethe's mind outside of her body" (Demetrakopoulos 53). Sethe's mind is initially not completely lost, although she no longer socializes with the outside world—she goes to town to work—and confines herself within the walls of 124 Bluestone Road, a house that by the time Beloved returns is inhabited only by women and is an example of a female realm. Thus, the text illustrates Sethe's radical cut from any possible interactions with the community. Her mind becomes a reminder of the atrocious past, and a limitation to seeing a better future. With Beloved's appearance, the situation worsens, since Sethe comes to understand that the daughter/ ghost embodies the "past that must be remembered in order to be forgotten; she symbolizes what must be reincarnated in order to be buried, properly" (Rushdy 571), a process she is not ready to initiate. Nonetheless, Beloved can be considered the possible embodiment of the resurrected daughter, as well as the embodiment of the collective pain of all enslaved African American women who died during the Middle Passage. Furthermore, Beloved can be seen as Sethe's punishment for the "moral decision" (Kwang 155) to kill the "crawling-already? girl" (Morrison, *Beloved* 110) and comes to symbolize Sethe's guilt and what "must be reincarnated in order to be buried, properly" (Rushdy 571). The text exemplifies a possible historical meaning for Beloved in the following passage:

Everybody knew what she was called, but nobody anywhere knew her name. Disremembered and unaccounted for, she cannot be lost because no one is looking for her, and even if they were, how can they call her if they don't know her name? Although she has claim, she is not claimed. (323)

Morrison and Knowledge

Up to recently, at the Nobel Museum in Stockholm, Sweden, it was possible to hear all the Nobel Prize laureates' speeches. In her speech, Morrison says, "[n]arrative has never been merely entertainment for me. It is, I believe, one of the principal ways in which we absorb knowledge" ("Morrison"). We can apply these words to the literary function of *Beloved*. The novel is not only entertainment, but a way for the author to convey knowledge, in this case, knowledge about slavery, African American women and men, and their lives during the Middle Passage, slavery, and afterwards. Therefore, if Morrison conveys her knowledge, facts, and feelings, readers absorb her knowledge. Furthermore, with her statement, the author places her work in a specific genre that can be viewed as more than fiction. Linda Hutcheon calls this genre "historiographic metafiction," since its aim is to "re-write or re-represent the past in fiction and in history" in order to "open it up to the present, to prevent it from being conclusive and teleological" ("Historiographic" 834). Kimberly Davis also adds that this genre is fiction-based and calls it the "fictionality of history." More importantly, according to Davis, this genre revises "our sense of what history can mean and accomplish" (K. Davis, "Postmodern" 242).

According to Jan Furman, Morrison's *Beloved* is an "instrument for transmitting cultural knowledge" (4). The cultural knowledge that Furman discusses resembles the parameters of postmodernism. However, as Davis maintains, Morrison "cannot be comfortably grouped alongside post-modern writers such as Milan Kundera or Thomas Pynchon" because her writing is more "concerned with reconstructing agency and subversive political content" (254). The narrative of *Beloved* begins with an historical event, followed by a journey causing the main female character to realize that she can obtain an audible voice. In so doing, Morrison writes "the voiceless black subaltern back into the history" (Kwang 154).

In the novel, an example of voiceless African Americans is found in Sixo, one of the male slaves at Sweet Home. Sixo does in fact stop "speaking English" (Morrison, *Beloved* 30) when he finally recognizes his powerless condition and decides to surrender to the power of the white master. He fights hard against the white supremacy and for this reason we can maintain that his act can be seen as a radical act of resistance making him the least cowed person at Sweet Home. As Rigney points out, the Black community was defined by the white, which consequently enforced "the black silence ... through the metaphoric and the actual insertion of the bit in the mouth" ("Breaking" 142). Coming to this realization, Sixo makes the choice of no longer speaking. By doing so, he expresses the impossibility of reaching vocal expression. However, later on when he is sent to be burned alive, he sings a song called "Seven-O" (Morrison, *Beloved* 270). Although knowing that he will never be able to see his and the Thirty-Mile Woman's child, he dies laughing, acknowledging that she was able to escape and eventually give birth to their child. By choosing not to speak, he is defiant until the end, which gives him a partial power over the institution of slavery. Morrison reveals many injustices in *Beloved*, stressing not only the physical abuses suffered by African Americans, but also their psychological devastation (Kwang 159).

According to Kim Kwang Soon, Morrison's works can be read "within the context of postcolonial theory which deconstructs Western cultural hegemony but still affirms a denied or alienated subjectivity and represents the lived experience of oppressed people" (3). In my view, the focus should instead be placed on the representation of Black female self-actualization and historical experience. This conforms to Morrison's statement that literature can be adopted as a way for readers to absorb knowledge. Morrison's works, and *Beloved* is a clear example, possess political meaning, since they describe the social and historical experience of an alienated racial group. The Blackness that emerges from Morrison's *Beloved* is a counter to whites' historical supremacy. It is an indispensable condition for the emergence of Black women's identity. Therefore, the text gives voice to those who could not speak during slavery, allowing them to undergo a process during and through which they recuperate their voices and develop the strength to speak for themselves. This is not an easy process, since these voices must fight against strongly implemented racial discourses: Black people are accused of being animals and savages by whites.

The journey that Black people initiate is not only against white supremacy, but also towards reconstitution of "Black identity in a multicultural context" (15). An example of the reconstitution of Black identity is found at the end of the novel, when Paul D returns to 124 Bluestone Road. He is not only alarmed by Sethe's psychological condition, but notices that she has given up on life. This can be connected to Sethe's escape from Sweet Home.

When on the run, Sethe finds herself with breasts full of milk for Beloved, and with a baby ready to be delivered. At this point, she is not willing to give up on life because she knows that her children need her, both the living ones and the baby soon to be born. Although the atrocities of her past return to her mind and heart, she is able to hold them at bay knowing that her children are safely waiting for her in Ohio. Unfortunately, the circumstances around her contribute to Sethe not knowing how to imagine her own future (Demetrakopoulos 53). Demetrakopoulos argues that "Sethe cannot participate in the ongoingness of life; she cannot imagine herself into history" (53–54). In the novel, her children are viewed as an "integral part of herself in an implication of ownership" (Mock 118). It is here that the word "ownership" raises complicated issues. A condition imposed on African American people during slavery was that a slave could not own anything. How can we then discuss ownership? This is possibly one of the most delicate problems depicted in the novel, since during slavery—both in the novel and in the real lives of African Americans—bodies, children, and milk were the property of the slaves' captors, who were the legal sole owners of these things.

Morrison focuses on the significance of milk. When Sethe is assaulted, and Schoolteacher's nephews take her milk—an act not narrated in detail—she does not direct her full attention to how this is done, but rather on the deprivation of her milk, which is for her children now living in Ohio. One reason for this could be that the retelling is too upsetting. Mary Jane Suero Elliott sees the theft of the milk as schoolteacher's discursive semblance, which "exploits Sethe as a racial and sexual other in order to re-write her identity as that of a subhuman creature, bestial rather than human" (185). By dehumanizing Sethe, schoolteacher emphasizes his ownership of another human being. He withholds her human values—the difference between a person and an animal—and makes sure Sethe understands the meaning of the act, although he does not show any compassion towards her. Schoolteacher thinks she is an animal. His intention is to deprive Sethe of the only source of humanity left in her: milk. Her milk is the only agency and power she has left as a mother. If it is taken away from her, her children will starve. At the same time, Sethe also reproduces this logic – she sees her children as entities that she owns – this is the dilemma–or one of them–of the novel.

Conclusion

As Timothy B. Powell observes, "Toni Morrison raises Afro-American fiction out of the black (w)hole, giving us instead a (w)holy black text"

(759). Eventually the stories narrated and heard provide clarity and understanding, both of which augment the intensity of the novel's rhythm. Bowers maintains that "[b]y speaking the horror, Morrison assumes and helps to create the community that can hear it and transform it" (75). The novel shows how enslavement reduces individuals to objects in the "external world," as well as fragmented selves in the "individual's internal world" (Schapiro 194). Sethe cannot allow her children to experience slavery. Thus, when explaining why she killed Beloved, Sethe explains, "[i] f I hadn't killed her she would have died and that is something I could not bear to happen to her" (Morrison, *Beloved* 236). Slavery killed the selves and bodies of many Black people. In *Beloved*, Morrison distinctly condemns the institution of slavery as well as its aftermath. She allows Sethe to claim back her own self in order to acquire agency, of which Black women and men were deprived during slavery. The reclaiming process Sethe undergoes in the novel gives her better prospects for the future. In addition, what it mostly gives her is speaking agency to recount the past in her own terms so the present becomes more bearable and planning the future more feasible. This process is unfortunately not easy. Perhaps this is why Morrison ends the novel with the word "Beloved," suggesting that "the past is a lasting presence, wanting to be resurrected" (K. Davis, *Postmodern* 251), and, as Sethe teaches us, "anything dead coming back to life hurts" (Morrison, *Beloved* 42).

Beloved is a literary masterpiece, partly due to the plot's structural organization. Morrison begins the narration by illustrating a little known historical event, which introduces the reader to the brutality of slavery; she then shifts the focus to the consequences of dismemberment among the Black female and male characters. Since slavery turned Black subjects into mere flesh, Morrison aims to re-allocate agency to these subjects—female subjects, specifically—and to transform them into remembering subjects. By displacing the attention to the psychological aftermath of slavery, Morrison provides a story to pass on so as not to let the unspeakable thoughts be left unspoken (*Beloved* 235).

Works Cited

Andrews, William L., and Nellie Y. McKay, eds. *Toni Morrison's Beloved: A Casebook*. Oxford: Oxford UP, 1999. Print.

Bast, Florian. "Reading Red: The Troping of Trauma in Toni Morrison's *Beloved*." *Callaloo* 34.4 (2011): 1069–86. Print.

Bowers, Susan. "*Beloved* and the New Apocalypse." *Journal of Ethnic Studies* 18.1 (1990): 59–77. Print.

Caesar, Terry Paul. "Slavery and Motherhood in Toni Morrison's 'Beloved.'" *Revista de Letras* 34 (1994): 111–20. Print.

David, Ron. *Toni Morrison Explained*. New York: Random House, 2000. Print.

Davis, Cynthia J. "Speaking the Body's Pain: Harriett Wilson's *Our Nig*." *African American Review* 27.3 (1993): 391–404. Print.

Davis, Kimberly Chabot. "'Postmodern Blackness': Toni Morrison's *Beloved* and the End of History." *Twentieth Century Literature* 44.2 (1998): 242–60. Print.

Demetrakopoulos, Stephanie A. "Maternal Bonds As Devourers of Women's Individuation in Toni Morrison's *Beloved*." *African American Review* 26.1 (1992): 51–59. Print.

Dobbs, Cynthia. "Toni Morrison's *Beloved*: Bodies Returned, Modernism Revisited." *African American Review* 32.4 (1998): 563–78. Print.

Elliott, Mary Jane Suero. "Postcolonial Experience in a Domestic Context: Commodified Subjectivity in Toni Morrison's *Beloved*." *MELUS* 24.3–4 (2000): 181–202. Print.

Fox-Genovese, Elizabeth. "Unspeakable Things Unspoken: Ghosts and Memories in *Beloved*." Bloom, *Modern Critical Interpretations: Toni* 97–114.

Furman, Jan. *Toni Morrison's Fiction*. Columbia: U of South Carolina P, 1996. Print.

Gourdine, Angeletta. "Hearing Reading and Being 'Read' by Beloved." *NWSA* 10.2 (1998): 13–31. Print.

hooks, bell. *Ain't I a Woman? Black Women and Feminism*. Boston: South End, 1981. Print.

—. "Beloved Community: A World without Racism." Steger and Lind 308–12.

—. *Feminist Theory: From Margin to Center*. Boston: South End, 1985. Print.

—. *Talking Back: Thinking Feminist Thinking Black*. Boston: South End, 1989. Print.

—. "Writing the Subject: Reading *The Color Purple*." Gates, *Reading* 454–71.

—. *Yearning: Race, Gender, and Cultural Politics*. Boston: South End, 1990. Print.

Hurston, Zora Neale. *Moses, Man of the Mountain*. 1939. New York: Harper, 2008. Print.

Hutcheon, Linda. "Historiographic Metafiction." McKeon 830–50.

Koolish, Linda. "'To Be Loved and Cry Shame': A Psychological Reading of Toni Morrison's *Beloved*." *MELUS* 26.4 (2001): 169–95. Print.

Kwang, Kim Soon. "The Location of Black Identity in Toni Morrison's Fiction." Diss. Purdue U, 2010. Print.

Lavon, Maxine Montgomery. *Conversations with Gloria Naylor*. Jackson: U of Mississippi P, 2004. Print.

McDermott, Ryan P. "Silence, Visuality and the Staying Image: The 'Unspeakable Scene' of Toni Morrison's *Beloved*." *Angelaki* 8.1 (2003): 75–88. Print.

McKeon, Michael, ed. *Theory of the Novel: A Historical Approach*. Baltimore: Johns Hopkins UP, 2000. Print.

Mock, Michele. "Spitting out the Seed: Ownership of Mother, Child, Breasts, Milk, and Voice in Toni Morrison's *Beloved*." *College Literature* 23.3 (1996): 117–26. Print.

Moglen, Helene. "Redeeming History: Toni Morrison's *Beloved*." *Cultural Critique* 24 (1993): 17–40. Print.

Morrison, Toni. *Beloved*. 1987. London: Vintage, 2005. Print.

—. "Toni Morrison Nobel Prize Acceptance Speech 1993." Stockholm Nobel Museum, Stockholm, Sweden.

Naylor, Gloria. "A Conversation: Gloria Naylor and Toni Morrison." Taylor-Guthrie 188–218.

Naylor, Gloria and Toni Morrison. "A Conversation." *Southern Review* 21.3 (1985): 567–93. Print.

Pal, Sunanda. "From Periphery to Centre: Toni Morrison's Self Affirming Fiction." *Economic and Political Weekly* 29.37 (1994): 2439–443. Print.

Pérez-Torres, Rafael. "Between Presence and Absence: Beloved: Postmodernism, and Blackness." Andrews and McKay 179–203.

Peterson, Nancy J. *Toni Morrison: Critical and Theoretical Approaches*. London: Johns Hopkins UP, 1997. Print.

Powell, Timothy B. "Toni Morrison: The Struggle to Depict the Black Figure on the White Page." *Black American Literature Forum* 24.4 (1990): 747–60. Print.

Rigney, Barbara Hill. "Breaking the Back of Words: Language, Silence and the Politics of Identity in *Beloved*." Solomon 138–47.

—. *The Voices of Toni Morrison*. Columbus: Ohio State UP, 1991. Print.

Robinson, Douglas. *American Apocalypses; The Image of the End of the World in Literature*. Baltimore: Johns Hopkins UP, 1968. Print.

Rushdy, Ashraf H. A. "Daughters Signifyin(g) History: The Example of Toni Morrison's *Beloved*." *American Literature* 64.3 (1992): 567–97. Print.

Schapiro, Barbara. "The Bonds of Love and the Boundaries of Self in Toni Morrison's *Beloved*." *Contemporary Literature* 32.2 (1991): 194–210. Print.

Suprajitno, Setefanus. "Reconstructing Womanhood in Toni Morrison's *Beloved*." *K@ta* 2.2 (2000): 60–64. Print.

Taylor-Guthrie, Danille, ed. *Conversations with Toni Morrison*. Jackson: U of Mississippi P, 1994. Print.

Van Der Zee, James, Owen Dodson, and Camille Billops, eds. *The Harlem Book of the Dead*. New York: Morgan and Morgan, 1978. Print.

—. "Foreword." Van Der Zee, Dodson, and Billops Foreword.

Wyatt, Jean. "Giving Body to the Word: The Maternal Symbolic in Toni Morrison's *Beloved*." *PMLA* 108.3 (1993): 474–88. Print.

The Black Mother as Murderess: William Faulkner's *Requiem for a Nun* and Toni Morrison's *Beloved*

Lucy Buzacott

In William Faulkner's 1950 novel *Requiem for a Nun*, a black woman employed by a white family to care for their children declares: "I've tried everything I knowed. You can see that" (168), and walks into room of the infant for whom she is employed to care and smothers her to death. The murder of this white child at the hands of her black caretaker is revelatory in that it turns the mammy figure on her head. The figure of the sexless, selfless, maternal mammy has long been a central trope in apologias for slavery and segregation in the American South. Arguably, mammy's most famous appearance in fiction is in Margaret Mitchell's *Gone with the Wind*, and her prevalence in fiction and popular culture continues, most recently in Kathryn Stockett's novel *The Help* and the subsequent movie adaptation. Faulkner's representation of Nancy Mannigoe, the mammy as murderess, complicates traditional versions of mammy. Far from the abundant and devoted mammy who tended to Scarlett O'Hara, here, in Faulkner's work is a mammy who enacts violence on the body of a white infant. This essay considers Nancy's murder of the white child in her care in conversation with Sethe's murder of her child in Toni Morrison's *Beloved*. What do these acts of infanticide reveal about black maternity during and after slavery and what changes when is not mother, but mammy that kills? These questions are bound to issues of black maternal potency and the agency of black women during and after slavery.

While both Nancy and Sethe murder a child in their care, their characterisations are, in many ways, vastly different. Sethe is an ex-slave, devoted to her biological children and cognisant of their precarious position within Southern society. Sethe kills her biological child, a baby girl, rather than see her return to slavery. Sethe's murder, whilst horrific, has been read by critics as an act of both maternal potency and maternal devotion. Sethe's murder is born out of her experience of slavery's horror and her desire to protect her child from these systems. In *Requiem*, Nancy Mannigoe is an ex-prostitute, ex-drug addict who murders not her biological child, but the white baby girl to whom she is mammy. Yet in Faulkner's novel, like Morrison's, Nancy's murder is to be understood as an act of love, rather than an act of violence. It is Gavin Stevens, Nancy's white lawyer, who, by the conclusion of the novel, has recast Nancy's act of infanticide as the ultimate sacrifice a black woman can make on behalf of the white family. Nancy has 'saved' the white child from her reckless mother by killing her.

Both *Beloved* and *Requiem* circle around the key act of infanticide. In both novels a black woman murders a child in her care and what follows is a dissection of black maternal grief, power, and love. Yet despite these similarities, very few critics have considered Sethe and Nancy's infanticide as comparative. One of the only studies to consider *Beloved* and *Requiem* is Doreen Fowler's "Reading for the 'Other Side': *Beloved* and *Requiem for a Nun*." Fowler highlights the similarities between Faulkner and Morrison's novels suggesting that in both,

> a mother or mother-surrogate kills an infant, not out of hate, but out of love. In both novels, the murderer-mother is black; in both novels, the infanticide is the central crisis which the novel ceaselessly investigates, casting forward and back for answers, seeking to see and know. (140)

Sethe murders Beloved to save her from entering the violent system of slavery, which is, of course, particularly dangerous for black women. And while Sethe's act of infanticide is itself horrific, her extreme actions are in response to the similarly extreme systems of which she is a part. As such, the suggestion that Sethe kills her child in order to "save" her and therefore, that the act of murder is interpreted as an act of love, holds. However, in *Requiem* the stakes are vastly different. The child Nancy kills is not her own, but the daughter of her white employee.

Fowler suggests that, like Sethe, Nancy murders the child in an act of love and certainly, this is the argument put forth by Gavin Stevens, and it is accepted by many critics of the novel, including Fowler. However, what is troubling about Gavin's defence of Nancy is that it considers a white child having an absent or ill-equipped mother as a fate worse than death. Nancy murders the white child because her mother, Temple Drake, is planning to

86

leave with her lover "children or no children", abandoning her older son and taking her infant daughter with her (*Requiem* 168). It is one thing to say that slavery is worse than death, in the case of *Beloved*, but it is another thing entirely to say that being the child of an unchaste white mother is also worse than death. Therefore, equating Nancy's murder with Sethe's as an act of maternal love is misleading. Instead, it is necessary to consider Nancy's action in conversation with the long history of mythologizing the mammy figure and to consider how her representation in *Requiem* in many ways drastically challenges, but ultimately conforms to the stereotypical version of mammy.

The mammy has long been a stock character in the landscape of Southern fiction; along with the Southern belle and the Southern gentleman, mammy promoted a distorted view of Southern history that reimagined slavery as a benign institution which comforted and supported happy slaves, who loyally served their noble white masters and pure white mistresses. Born out of such a tradition, the mammy was the exemplary "happy slave" figure—loyal, loving, fat, devoted, sexless, maternal. The stereotypic mammy is wholly devoted to the white family who employs her and the white children for whom she cares. As such, a mammy who murders a white child is an astonishing break from her mythical ancestors and sisters. Indeed, the notion of a mammy who murders is something that the rich and varied literature concerning mammy has considered very rarely.

Kimberley Wallace-Sanders in *Mammy: A of Race, Gender and Southern Memory*, cites only one example of a murderess mammy and calls this depiction "unique" (112). The murdering mammy that Wallace-Sanders considers appears in Adeline Ries's 1917 short story "Mammy: A Story." Wallace-Sanders argues that "in the array of mammies from the nineteenth to the twentieth centuries [Ries's] unique depiction of a killer or brute mammy seems to have appeared and disappeared in silence" (112). Wallace-Sanders does not consider, or even mention Faulkner's rendition of the killer mammy in *Requiem* despite the fact that at other points her argument considers other Faulknerian mammies. Why does Wallace-Sanders skip over Nancy? Is it because her murder is reimagined by Stevens at the end of the novel as less about black subjectivity and more about black sacrifice on the altar of whiteness? The critical silence surrounding Nancy's murder of her mistress Temple Drake's child reiterates the slipperiness of Faulkner's portrayal of the murdering mammy. Nancy is the black mother made potent through an act of violence, yet she is not actually mother but mammy and her potency in Faulkner's hands only succeeds in bolstering the white family.

In Ries's story the (always unnamed) mammy's biological daughter is sold away to the white woman who she has raised. Mammy's biological daughter is sold to the white woman to become a mammy to the white woman's child. The mammy then murders the infant daughter of the white woman she had raised after her biological daughter dies. The story ends with the mammy tossing the white baby into the ocean and:

> hours later, two slaves in frantic search for the missing child found Mammy on the beach tossing handfuls of sand into the air and uttering loud, incoherent cries. And as they came close, she pointed towards the sea and with the laugh of a mad-woman shouted: "They took her from me an' she died!" (523)

Wallace-Sanders suggests that in Ries's story "the symbol of racial harmony [that is, the mammy] is distorted until the fantasy and myth dissolves into a tragic nightmare" (110). And that "Ries exploits our expectation that the mammy's grief, and ostensibly any slave mother's grief, is impotent. She then provides a lesson in subversion by reminding her readers that sometimes there are no black children to whom the mammy can return" (111).

Can we read Nancy like Ries's mammy? That is, can we read her murder as part of a genealogy of black maternity outraged by slavery and its aftermath? Such a rendering would align Nancy's act with both Ries's mammy and Morrison's Sethe. Nancy appears to have no biological children of her own in *Requiem*, but what is rarely mentioned by critics of the novel is that Nancy has been pregnant at least once and lost the baby she as carrying as a result of extreme violence at the hands of a nameless white man. A man who, when confronted by Nancy for payment for her services as a prostitute—was asked "where's my two dollars white man?" (*Requiem* 110)—then "struck her, knocked her across the pavement into the gutter and then ran after her, stomping and kicking at her face" until she was "spitting blood and teeth and still saying "it was two dollars more than two weeks ago and you done been back twice since" (*Requiem* 110). While the novel does not make it clear that Nancy is pregnant here and loses her child as a result of this attack, later in the novel her miscarried child is brought up by Temple Drake, her white employer, who asks her about the child she was carrying "six months gone" where she "went to a picnic or dance or frolic or fight or whatever it was, and the man kicked you in the stomach and you lost it?" (*Requiem* 245). Nancy's position as an ex-prostitute complicates her role as mammy—here is the mammy who is also Jezebel—that other problematic rendition of black femininity promoted by the white South. Nancy's sexuality and her fertility are outside the boundaries of the traditional mammy who is both deeply maternal but essentially sexless.

So how does Nancy's miscarriage change the way we view her murder of Temple's baby? It certainly does not change the fact that the act of infanticide itself is abhorrent, but it does complicate the way that Nancy's maternity can be read. Returning to Ries's "Mammy: A Story", Wallace-Sanders argues that "mammy's biological motherhood is repeatedly denied, leaving her powerless to protect her child" (112). Similarly, criticism of *Beloved* has cited Sethe's maternal powerlessness and her infanticide as an attempt to enact maternal potency. Marianne Hirsh suggests that "when Sethe tries to explain to Beloved why she cut her throat, she is explaining an anger handed down through generations of mothers who could have no control over their children's lives, no voice in their upbringing" (196). It is therefore the notion of powerlessness or impotence regarding their maternity that is central to considerations of black maternal infanticide. As such, the "silent act of infanticide serves as a vehicle through which the marginal mother can speak" (Harvey 12). Fowler analogises Nancy's act to Sethe's and argues that "in *Requiem* as in *Beloved* the mother-child bond is under attack" (142). But this reading fails to take into account the troubling fact that the 'mother-child bond' is determined to be 'under attack' in *Requiem* because of the white mother's sexual transgressions. While in *Beloved* Sethe is trying to save her daughter from the horrors of slavery which she has herself experienced first-hand, Nancy's murder is ultimately about reinstating the fallen white woman back onto her pedestal.

So is it possible to consider Nancy's murder of the white baby as connected to the loss of her own child, likely at the hands of a white man? *Requiem* does not make clear that Nancy acts out of revenge – she does not, like Ries's Mammy, actively murder because of her own lost child. But that does not mean that the two dead babies in the novel (the unnamed white child and the miscarried child) are not in some way connected. Nancy reveals the problem of maternity for the black woman in the South, particularly when the black woman is both mammy and mother. And while Nancy's position as mother is never fully realized (although, her history is so sketchy that other children are possible), there still exists in her character the tension of dispossessed black maternity, more fully realized in texts like Morrison's and Ries's.

The picture of Nancy Mannigoe that emerges from her actions in *Requiem* is a mammy who is deeply and troublingly transgressive. Nancy is, in the words of Temple Drake and other white characters in the novel, a "whore" mammy whose troubling maternal potential is fully realized when she smothers a white infant in its crib. Nancy's position as an ex-prostitute, ex-drug addict mammy who murders a child in her care, outwardly compromises her ability to become idealised under the same terms as other fictional versions of mammy. However, by the end of *Requiem* the murdering Jezebel mammy has been recast by Gavin Stevens as a definitive figure of transcendent black maternity. As Paradiso has argued, Nancy has no "place" within the Southern society of Yoknapatwpha as a "reformed prostitute who murders in the name of the lord." But, Paradiso continues, "the people in the form of Gavin Stevens... find a way to make her fit: by turning her into a saint" (29).

Gavin needs to rationalise Nancy's actions in such a way that will not destabilise the sanctity of the white family. Readers are not led to consider Nancy's murder as stemming from hate, anger, or madness; instead, by the end of the novel, her murder is coded in terms of black sacrifice. By the end of the novel Gavin has successfully returned Temple Drake, the fallen Southern belle and mother of the murdered child, to her position as mother within the white family, and in doing so, has exalted Nancy to a position of saintly black sacrifice.

Nancy's murder is cast as a deliberate double sacrifice of the white child and herself so that she may save the white woman and her family. Nancy herself is resigned to her own death, speaking of it as "pay for the suffering" (*Requiem* 242). She "just believes" in God and his path and her death is presented as simply part of the transaction required to purchase redemption for herself and the white family she is ultimately shown to serve. Nancy's murder of the white child and her subsequent execution is recast by Gavin Stevens as the ultimate sacrifice of the black mammy for the white family. Stevens tells Temple Drake that Nancy "will die tomorrow to postulate that little children, as long as they are little children, shall be intact, unanguished, untorn, unterrified" (*Requiem* 185). Gavin's reading of the murder of Temple's child iterates that for him, being the child of a sexually impure mother is worse than death. Nancy has protected Temple's remaining child from anguish and terror by murdering his infant sister, Stevens argues. This makes no sense, but in Faulkner's South such an argument holds. Stevens does not consider for even a moment that the death of his sister would cause anguish or terror for the remaining child. Instead, having his mother returned to her pedestal as Southern lady and mother is more important than the life of the murdered infant, or indeed, the life of the mammy.

The black mammy is sanctified in *Requiem* because of her sacrifice to the white family. The double sacrifice of white baby and black mammy is committed, Gavin Stevens insists, because holding together a white family is the essential goal for the black mammy. In *Requiem*, a black woman, a mammy, gives everything of herself so that whiteness is preserved. How might we come to terms with this distinctly problematic exchange? I want to consider the characterisation of Nancy in conversation with another exchange, one that occurred in 1956 between William Faulkner and James Baldwin. In February of 1956 Faulkner gave an interview to William Howe in which he espoused a variety of controversial views regarding segregation. In response to this interview James Baldwin wrote an article titled "Faulkner and Desegregation" in which he roundly criticised Faulkner's position regarding race relations. While "Faulkner and Desegregation" does not consider *Requiem*, Baldwin does consider *Requiem* elsewhere. In *No Name in the Street* Baldwin speaks of *Requiem*'s conclusion and asks "why Faulkner may have needed to believe in a black forgiveness?" (380). This question is central to Baldwin's concerns about *Requiem* but also to the more general concerns he highlights in "Faulkner and Desegregation". In his infamous interview Faulkner encouraged civil right activists to "go slow" (*Lion* 258) in taking steps toward racial equality. Baldwin, in his critique of Faulkner's criticizes Faulkner's suggestion that "white Southerners, left to their own devices, will realize that their own social structure looks silly to the rest of the world and correct it of their own accord" (*Faulkner* 148), but, Baldwin argues, they have instead "clung to it, at incalculable cost to themselves, as the only conceivable and as an absolutely sacrosanct way of life" (148).

Faulkner insists that Southerners simply require more time, that civil rights activists and Northerners need to "take the pressure off" the white South and let them come around to equality in their own time and on their own terms (*Lion* 249). This "wait and see" attitude, the call to "go slow" is not enough for Baldwin, who asks "just what Negroes are supposed to do while the South works out what, in Faulkner's rhetoric, becomes something very closely resembling a high and noble tragedy" (*Faulkner* 148). Baldwin argues that the essential feature of Faulkner's rhetoric regarding race is that his concerns are about white people, rather than black. Specifically, Baldwin suggests that the defeat of the South by the North left the South with only one means "of asserting its identity and that means was the negro" (*Faulkner* 151). As such, white Southerners are reliant on African Americans to define themselves. Ann Anlin Cheng in *The Melancholy of Race* suggests that "segregation and colonialism are internally fraught institutions not because they have eliminated the Other but because they need the very thing they hate or fear" (12). The white South does not wish to eliminate blacks, for without them how would they know themselves? Instead, they must recast the racial situation. For Faulkner, his view that the white South is in some way inevitably damned and blacks already saved, leads him to idealise blackness to the point of unreality, sanctifying black suffering through characterisations such as Nancy's murdering mammy. This racial set up, whites as doomed and blacks as saved, is deeply problematic because it fails to allow for a scenario in which blacks can be anything other than martyrs.

Faulkner places himself on the side of equality but advocates a moderate plan forward. However, Faulkner is thinking of whites rather than blacks when he advocates for a slow and gradual process of desegregation. Faulkner tells Howe,

> we know that racial discrimination is morally bad, that it stinks, that it shouldn't exist, but it does. Should we obliterate the persecutor by acting in a way that we know will send him to his guns, or should we compromise and let it work out in time and save whatever good remains in those white people? (*Lion* 261)

A program of compromise and gradual gains whose end result would be to save whatever good remains in whites is understandably inadequate to commentators like Baldwin who have suffered the continuing ravages of racial inequality. It is hard to imagine how going slow might comfort blacks for whom Southern history has been, in Baldwin's words, "an intolerable yoke, a stinking prison, a shrieking grave" (*No Name* 380). Baldwin interprets Faulkner's desire to save "whatever good remains in these white people" as an indication that he believes that Negroes are therefore "already saved" (*Faulkner* 152). The Negroes, Baldwin continues "who, having refused to be destroyed by terror, are far stronger than the terrified white populace" (*Faulkner* 152). Faulkner seems to think that because of their suffering, blacks are able to claim the high moral ground and he seems to be suggesting that such a position is an adequate substitute for a life lived without fear and prejudice. It is white moral identity that is at risk in Faulkner's reading of the South. Baldwin's reading of Faulkner here can be applied to his representation of Nancy who, despite her horrific, violent actions is 'already saved' at the conclusion of the novel. Nancy does not need to be saved, but she will sacrifice everything of herself in order to save 'whatever good remains' in the white people around her—particularly her white mistress Temple Drake.

Ultimately, both Sethe and Nancy's acts of infanticide speak to the disempowerment of black women in the South both during and after slavery. However, while Sethe's murder can be coded as an attempt to gain some form of maternal potency by a woman rendered impotent by her social, racial, and gendered place, the idealisation of Nancy's murder in *Requiem* becomes problematic because it apotheosises a black woman for her imagined sacrifice to whites. So while the murder of an infant is undoubtedly horrific in any case, Sethe's action is part of a wider system of violence and oppression which aims to destroy black families and while this does not excuse her actions, it does go some way toward explaining them. And while Nancy is similarly dispossessed due to her race, gender, and social and sexual status, the motives behind her murder are less clear and the novel's explanation of Nancy becomes mythologising and her murder becomes yet another instance of the mammy sacrificing her own body in support of the white family.

Works Cited

Baldwin, James. "Faulkner and Desegregation". *The Price of the Ticket: Collected Non-Fiction 1948–1985*. London: Michael Joseph, 1985. 147–152.

—. 'No Name in the Street". *James Baldwin: Collected Essays*. New York: Library of America, 1998. 350–475.

Cheng, Ann Anlin. *The Melancholy of Race*: *Psychoanalysis, Assimilation, and Hidden Grief*. New York: Oxford, 2001.

Faulkner, William. *Requiem for a Nun*. 1950. New York: Vintage, 1996.

—. "Interview with Russell Howe". 1956. *Lion in the Garden: Interviews with William Faulkner*. Ed. James B. Meriwether and Michael Millgate. London: U of Nebraska P, 1980. 257–264.

Fowler, Doreen. "Reading for the "Other Side": *Beloved* and *Requiem for a Nun*." *Unflinching Gaze: Morrison and Faulkner Re-Envisioned*. Eds. Carol

A. Kolmerten, Judith Bryant Wittenberg. Jackson: UP of Mississippi, 1997. 139–151.

Harvey, Brandy Andrews. *After the Silence: Narrating Infanticide as the Agent/Mother*. Dissertation. Lafayette: University of Louisana, 2007.

Hirsch, Marianne. *The Mother/Daughter Plot: Narrative, Psychoanalysis, Feminism*. Bloomington: Indiana UP, 1989.

Morrison, Toni. *Beloved*. 1986. London: Vintage, 2007.

Paradiso, Sharon Desmond. "Terrorizing Whiteness in Yoknapatawpha Country" *Faulkner Journal*. 3.2. 2008. 23–44.

Ries, Adeline F. "Mammy, A Story." *Short Fiction by Black Women, 1900–1920*. Ed. E. Ammons. New York: Oxford UP, 1991. 520–523.

Wallace-Sanders, Kimberly. *Mammy: A Century of Race, Gender, and Southern Memory*. Ann Arbor: Michigan UP, 2008.

A Valediction Forbidding Mo'nin?:
Beloved Revisited

Hilary Emmett

In subtitling this essay "*Beloved* Revisited" I seek to gesture to Toni Morrison's novel as a site, like Sweet Home, from which it is difficult to move on. My title also implies that, like traumatic memory, much of what is said about it may be in danger of being repetitive, evidence of a kind of stasis and failure to work through and move on. Indeed, it signals a lot of my own anxieties about whether there is anything new to say about *Beloved*. A perusal of the MLA listings shows that while the novel is not on par with *Hamlet*, or *Paradise Lost* as the most analysed text in the English language, or even *Ulysses* in relation to texts of the twentieth century, in relation to other modern American texts it stands in a class almost of its own, trumping major works by Faulkner, Ellison, Fitzgerald, Hemingway in terms of critical attention. The question to be asked, therefore, is: can we even talk about revisiting, if in fact we have never left?

What makes the account of *Beloved* that follows a "re-visitation" is that I want to use it to open up a pathway to return to a term that had enjoyed celebration, been subject to trenchant critique, and then suffered disposal around the same time that Beloved was coming into being and enjoying its first extraordinary outpourings of critical response in the early 1990s. This term is sisterhood—a designation that was embraced in the 1970s, put under the microscope in the 1980s, and then laid to rest in a series of post-mortems about its failures in the early 1990s, as evidenced by a proliferation of publications with titles such as *Segregated Sisterhood: Racism and the Politics of American Feminism* (1991), and even *Feminist Nightmares: Women at Odds—Feminism and The Problem of Sisterhood* (1994). I am interested in sisterhood as a category that has been relatively neglected in literary studies of the past twenty years, too easily subsumed into discussions of gender in general, and too readily dismissed as a naïve political affiliation. Indeed, what many theorists of the genesis of the liberal-democratic nation state describe as the exclusion of women in general from the public body politic, is in fact a failure to account for the place of the sister in the "imagined fraternity" of American citizenship.[1] Even analyses that critique the discourse of biological determinism which excludes women from the citizenry,[2] or trouble the rigidly gendered and aligned binaries of private/public, feminine/masculine,[3] often reproduce the logic of biological determinism by occluding the ways in which women themselves occupy a number of different positions within the generalized category of "womanhood." The very appropriation of the term "sisterhood" by feminism as a crucial component of its politics and vocabulary performs an identical move of converting the particularity of sisters into a universalized class of "women."

So what does the problem of sisterhood have to do with *Beloved*, a novel almost over-determined by its exploration of motherhood at its limit? There are two ways in which I think *Beloved* is a necessary text for re-thinking sisterhood. First, I think it is necessary to consider *Beloved* as a novel of traumatic sisterhood as well as a novel about traumatized maternity. And while I cannot claim to have read the nearly 700 entries on the MLA database, I have not yet come across an adequate account of the relationship between Beloved and Denver that is not triangulated via Sethe and does not consider them as the two daughters of one woman.[4] I realize that that could be understood as the very definition of sisterhood—the two daughters of a shared parent—but it also downplays the relationality of siblings to each other outside of their relationship to their parents. The second reason is the response my interest in sisterhood in American fiction often generates in academic circles; I regularly receive variations on the dismissal "It just sounds like bad 80s feminism!" when the word sisterhood is mentioned. For some time I adapted my terminology so that sisterhood became kinship à la Judith Butler, but the question that still plagues me: what is so bad about

---

[1] The phrase is Dana Nelson's from National Manhood: Capitalist Citizenship and the Imagined Fraternity of White Men (Durham: Duke University Press, 1998).

[2] See, for example, Lauren Berlant, "The Subject of True Feeling: Pain, Privacy and Politics" in *Cultural Studies and Political Theory*, Jodi Dean (ed.) (Ithaca: Cornell University Press, 2000), 42-62.

[3] Such as Elizabeth Maddock Dillon's *The Gender of Freedom: Fictions of Liberalism and the Literary Public Sphere* (Stanford: Stanford University Press, 2004).

[4] See, for example Connie R. Schomburg, "To Survive Whole, To Save the Self" in JoAnna Stephens Mink and Janet Doubler Ward, *The Significance of Sibling Relationships in Literature* (Bowling Green: Bowling Green State University Popular Press, 1992): 149-57.

80s feminism? Was it bad because it elided difference, and was therefore rightly taken to task by feminists such as bell hooks and others?[5] Or is it bad because it implies an excess of affect both mealy-mouthedly positive or corrosively, competitively negative? If this is the case, then, why is the term sisterhood still so avoided such that even Lauren Berlant in her examination of the affective origins and investments of women's culture does not acknowledge it as a significant rhetorical object of study?[6]

What I aim to show with the following reading that privileges the role of Denver as sister, is that *Beloved* is a novel that dramatizes the vexed operations of sisterhood in antebellum America. What I want to suggest ultimately, though this is beyond the scope of this essay, is that if we adhere to Walter Benjamin's insistence that "every image of the past must be recognized by the present as one of its own concerns" (247) or more specifically, if we accept Asharaf Rushdy's compelling arguments about the contemporary politics of neo-slave narrative (3–53), *Beloved* equally stages an intervention into the politics of cross-racial communitas in the 1980s.

I begin my account of the novel from the point at which Sethe, Beloved, and Denver have become locked in a melancholic stasis confined to 124. The three women engage in a fractured and fissured dialogue and as the conversation unfolds, their three voices become barely distinguishable from one another. Rising to a crescendo, it culminates in the repetition of the phrase "you are mine" (217). Mine. The word becomes the only one recognizable as the voices of the women merge with the indecipherable voices of "the black and angry dead" (199) that surround the house.

The women are thus cloaked by a wall of sound more impenetrable than any bolted door; as Denver describes it, "locked in a love that wore everybody out" (243). In recognizing this, Denver also recognizes that it is up to her to enact her own and her mother's transition from the twilight world of Beloved back into the land of the living. Snatched from "the arch of [her] mother's swing" by Stamp Paid (149), Denver's very existence is predicated on the community's denial of Sethe's right to control the fate of her children. It falls to her, therefore, to mediate between her mother and the

---

[5] See, for example, bell hooks' *Ain't I a Woman: Black Women and Feminism* (London: Pluto Press, 1982) and "Sisterhood: Political Solidarity Between Women" in Anne McClintock et al., *Dangerous Liaisons: Gender, Nation, and Postcolonial Perspectives* (Minneapolis: U of Minnesota P, 1997): 396-411. See also Sandra Kumamoto Stanley (ed.), *Other Sisterhoods: Literary Theory and U.S. Women of Color* (Urbana and Chicago: University of Illinois, 1998).

[6] I am thinking here of The Female Complaint: The Unfinished Business of Sentimentality in American Culture (Durham: Duke University Press, 2008).

"colored people" of Cincinnati. Yet she remains paralyzed by fear of a past that inheres in the present. Having made her decision to seek help from the community, she stands on the porch unable to move for dread of "the places where time didn't pass, where…the bad was waiting for her as well" (244). In her moment of hesitation, Baby Suggs' voice comes to her out of this past, reminding her of her family's immense capacity for survival. She encourages Denver to remember her mother's endurance, when, pregnant with Denver and running from schoolteacher, she kept herself alive for her children's sake. She acknowledges that Sethe's action was indefensible, but Denver is to accept the event as another devastating effect of slavery—as part of a catalogue of brutality that includes Baby Suggs' lameness, her father's disappearance and her mother's mutilated back. Recognizing this, Denver steps out of the yard and into the community.

Her mother's daughter still in that "asking for help from strangers was worse than hunger" (248), Denver nevertheless learns to accept the gifts of food and companionship offered by the women of the town. In doing so, she offsets her mother's pride and sets in motion both the bridging process between Sethe and the community, and her own development into a sovereign subject, an "owned self." Following a paper trail of "scraps containing […] handwritten names" (248) Denver painstakingly retraces the steps taken into her own yard by others, returning their plates and bowls and dishtowels and receiving in turn conversation. Her "soft thank-yous" prompt reminiscences of Baby Suggs, her preaching in the Clearing, her tonics for sick relatives, her soup, her largesse. And in remembering again "the party with twelve turkeys and tubs of strawberry smash," the women agree that "the personal pride, the arrogant claim staked at 124 seemed to them to have run its course" (249).

As the situation worsens, Denver resolves to appeal to the Bodwins for help. They had helped her family twice, she rationalizes, "once for Baby Suggs and once for her mother. Why not the third generation as well?" (252). The abolitionist Bodwins are the owners of the house on Bluestone Rd given over to Baby Suggs and her family following the purchase of her freedom. They were also instrumental in securing Sethe's release from prison and her subsequent employment at Sawyer's restaurant. But in appealing to the Bodwins she must ignore other words of Baby Suggs'; she must *selectively remember*:

"They got me out of jail," Sethe once told Baby Suggs.
"They also put you in it," she answered.

"They drove you 'cross the river."
"On my son's back."
"They gave you this house."
"Nobody *gave* me nothing."
"I got a job from them."
"He got a cook from them, girl" (244).

The Bodwins are in many ways profoundly ambivalent figures; they supplied clothing and housing for runaways, but only because "they hated slavery more than they hated the slaves" (137). Their black housekeeper, Janey, agrees that they are "good whitefolks" but even in her eyes this is a damning with faint praise. Denver accepts the offer of employment the Bodwins offer her, but not without knowledge of the racial superiority they feel. Like a kind of household god guarding the back door of the Bodwins' house sits

> a black boy's mouth, full of money. His head was thrown back, farther than a head could go, his hands were shoved in his pockets. Bulging like moons, two eyes were all the face he had above the gaping red mouth. His hair was a cluster of raised, widely spaced dots made of nail heads. And he was on his knees. His mouth, wide as a cup, held the coins needed to pay for a delivery or some other small service, but could just as well have held buttons or pins or crabapple jelly. Painted across the pedestal he knelt on were the words "At Yo Service." (255)

This figure obviously suggests the Bodwins' implication in a system of monetary exchange across black bodies, and also foregrounds an inter- estingly repeated image of the abuse of black male bodies. The kneeling black man has been encountered already in this novel. Paul D and his fellow members of the chain gang are forced to kneel before the white guards and offered the choice of a nauseating "breakfast" or a gunshot to the head: "the price of taking a bit of foreskin […] to Jesus" (108). The violence of this exploitation is clear in both cases. In the one, the threat of the gunshot is enough to keep men on their knees. In the other forced submission is implied in the hands "shoved" into binding pockets, the head wrenched back unnaturally, "farther than a head could go," the eyes bulging like moons due to the choking bulk of the metal weighing in the mouth. The money's weight also recalls the bit placed in Paul D's mouth, his "offended" tongue and "how the need to spit is so deep you cry for it"; the bulging eyes and gaping mouth recall "the wildness that shot up into the eye the moment the lips were yanked back" (71).

Violence, exploitation and degradation thus reside alongside whiteness in the Bodwin household. The Bodwins will employ Denver but she will pay them in return by having to share her story—"a little thing to pay, but it seemed big to Denver. Nobody was going to help her unless she told it, told all of it" (253). The price of her initiation into the black community and the white economy is the story of Beloved: what she is and how she came to be. That it is Janie to whom she must tell the story to brings these two things into undeniable relation with one another. Denver is right to see this price as significant in that telling Beloved's story paves the way for her sister's ultimate disappearance from the community. As the collapsing of title and character in this novel suggests, Beloved *is* her story. Denver pays this price precisely because she recognizes that Beloved cannot continue to exact an account from their mother. In giving away the family secret, Denver does, in a way, sell Beloved out. But her action is neither entirely one nor the other. Rather, she returns to the economy of sacrifice that Sethe failed fully to perform at the moment of her original infanticide.[7] A sacrifice is a gift of great price that elicits something in return; Denver sacrifices Beloved in return for the possibility of community, and a place within it.

In agreeing to work for the Bodwins, Denver sets the scene for a final re-configured re-enactment of the original infanticide. Despite her documented terror that "the thing that makes it all right to kill [...] children" might "come back into the yard" (206), she arranges for Edward Bodwin to collect her from the porch steps and take her to begin her employment in his house. Denver knows and fears her mother's capabilities but nevertheless arranges for a white man to encroach upon their yard. She knows that Sethe has been willing to kill once before to protect her child; does she hope that she will do so again? Sure enough, when Sethe sees Edward Bodwin approaching her house to collect Denver for work, she once again reaches for a weapon. But this time the ice-pick is not raised against her child, but against the white man whom she perceives to be the representative of those who caused her original suffering. As Sethe lunges towards Bodwin, Ella and Denver wrest the weapon from her grip before she can do him any harm. Simultaneously, the rest of the women of the town gather

---

[7] On Sethe's infanticide as a vexed act of sacrifice see Hilary Emmett, "The Maternal Contract in *Beloved* and *Medea*," in Anne Simon & Heike Bartel (eds), *Unbinding Medea: Interdisciplinary Approaches to a Classical Myth from Antiquity to the 21st Century*, (Oxford: Legenda Press, 2010): 248-260.

around the house and begin their exorcism of Beloved. As they assemble, a wave of sound surrounds the house. It is non-speech, yet it is not barbaric non-sense. Rather, it is understood by all who hear it to be a wordless threnody by which the death of Beloved, and her mother's part in it, are acknowledged, forgiven and mourned by the collective at last. This sound is also a literary rendering of Fred Moten's theorization of sound and mourning in which he posits the "wordless moan" as a means of vocalizing the ineffable. For Moten, the "mo'n" (the moan which mourns) "renders mourning wordless," but in doing so, "augments" it by "releasing more than what is bound up in the presence of the word" (73). "Words can't begin to tell you, but maybe moaning will" (Moten, 60). We might also hear in the *moan* a new note that converts the discordant cry of *mine* into a harmony of possession claimed and recognized, but in being so, must now be let go.

And so Beloved disappears. Memorably, "disremembered and unaccounted for" until she is "just weather. Certainly no clamour for a kiss." "You think she sure 'nough your sister?" Paul D asks Denver. "At times. At times I think she was—more," Denver replies (266). Denver's understanding of Beloved as her sister, and as signifying something "more" is revealing in that it both raises the question of what sisterhood might have meant in the immediate aftermath of slavery's abolition and gestures to sisterhood's excess, its unconfineable significance in United States' history. As many have argued, the something "more" that Beloved embodies is the uncontainability of the traumatic memory of slavery, the eternally recurring "rememory" which cannot be kept at bay, and as such, inhibits the free and forward movement of the community of former slaves. Such rememory repeats itself precisely because it cannot be narrativized. Yet while Morrison's novel lends itself well to readings that posit the direct causal relationship between trauma and the impossibility of narrative, there is another, more historically specific reason for the need to keep Beloved out of the community's shared story.

As Morrison herself has emphasized, *Beloved* was written with the intention of revealing what lay behind what Lydia Maria Child termed the "veil" drawn over the most "monstrous features" of slavery (7–8). Despite Child's rhetoric, the alliance forged between "conscientious and reflecting [white] women at the North" and their "sisters in bondage" was predicated on the slave narrator's elision of details that might prove too indelicate for white women's ears. As Jacqueline Goldsby and others have so ably shown, concealment, falsehood and subterfuge were not only the political strategies by which "Linda Brent" effects her liberation from bondage, but are also the discursive modes through which Harriet Jacobs transcribes her experience (11–12), leading to, in Saidiyah Hartman's words, the "seduction" of white, Northern women readers into identification with the slave woman (106–7). The rhetoric of sisterhood was deployed by abolitionist movements in both Britain and America, both to insist upon the common humanity of slaves, and to harness the momentum of the abolitionist cause to movements calling for women's rights—an alliance that would cause consternation among advocates of the cause of women's suffrage.[8] Sojouner Truth's alleged clarion call for the recognition of her womanhood, "Ain't I a Woman?" tapped into such rhetoric in its echo of the motto attached to Josiah Wedgwood's widely disseminated anti-slavery medallion. One of the most compelling images of the transatlantic abolitionist movement, the cameo commissioned by Wedgwood in 1788 depicted a kneeling slave in chains and carried the caption, "Am I not a Man and a Brother?" The 1828 version, portraying a suppliant female slave was accompanied by a scroll proclaiming, "Am I not a Woman and a Sister?"

Truth's testimony, which comes to us via the words of Frances Gage, written 30 years after the event, was apparently delivered to initially ambivalent effect at the 1851 Women's Rights Convention in Akron, Ohio (not far from Lorain, where Morrison herself was born and raised). Gage described the palpable (and vocal) unease which met Truth's now famous demand for equality with men, and more significantly, with white women on the levels of sentiment, labor, and maternity. In Gage's account, Truth's preparation to take the stage was met with entreaties from the more "timorous and trembling" proponents of suffrage not to align their cause "with abolition and niggers," and a "hissing sound of disapprobation" spread throughout the hall as she rose to give her testimony (cited in Stanton et al., 116). While Gage's version of the event concludes with her insistence that Truth's words turned the tide of public opinion in favor of abolition *and* women's rights, we also take away from this account the ready disavowal of the common sisterhood of black and white women by those for whom such a position is inherently distasteful.

---

[8] Also worth noting here is bell hooks' requisitioning of this phrase as the title of her 1981 exposition of the weak links in the alliance between civil rights activists and white feminists. The resurfacing of Truth's words at this particular political moment underscores my contention that *Beloved* is as much a novel about the ongoing trauma of sisterhood as it is about black maternity: both antebellum and post-Moynihan. bell hooks, *Ain't I a Woman?: Black Women and Feminism* (Boston: South End Press, 1981), 141.

My own emphasis on the position of Beloved as sister indexes a similar necessity among black "sisters." The moan that both mourns Beloved's death and acknowledges the community's implication in it simultaneously effects her erasure. As the embodiment of all the "unspeakable thoughts, unspoken" (199) of all the "black and angry dead" Beloved has no ongoing place in the community. Beloved is forgotten as a result of the ritual that called the women together for the first time since Baby Suggs' party:

> those that saw her that day on the porch quickly and deliberately forgot her. It took longer for those who had spoken to her, lived with her, fallen in love with her, to forget, until they realized they couldn't remember or repeat a single thing she had said. [...] So in the end, they forgot her too. Remembering seemed unwise. (274)

Each person, some with more alacrity than others, thus eventually commits to amnesia for the good of the community.

In her essay "Of Amnesty and its Opposite" Nicole Loraux references the Athenian "decree of amnesty" of 403 BCE. This declaration of an end to civil war required that citizens swear the oath: "I shall not recall the misfortunes." Loraux's essay investigates the etymological link between amnesty and amnesia implied by such an oath (84, 87). She argues that civic community can only be reconstituted through an individual commitment to deliberate forgetting. Such a collective conformity an institutionalized forgetting seems to explain why Beloved's story is "not a story to pass on." However, this phrase, repeated three times at the novel's close, as though it is an incantation, jars with the fact that Beloved's story has been recorded as text. The story that was not to be passed on has been concretized for posterity in a lasting cultural artifact. There are numerous critical accounts of this phrase that seek to reconcile the presence of this text with its injunction against repetition, most concluding that the ambiguity of the closing lines of the text reflects the psychic processes of mourning.

Mae Henderson argues that "pass on" may be read as a pun on the word pass: "this is not a story to be PASSED ON," in the sense that it is not to be repressed, forgotten or ignored (83). This reading is sustained by Sethe's conversation with Denver towards the beginning of the novel in which she comments, "I was talking about time. It's so hard for me to believe in it. Some things go. Pass on. Others just stay" (36). Here, "pass" quite clearly refers to a passage into oblivion, "passing away" as a euphemism for death.

Yet to resolve the ambiguity of this phrase too neatly is to totalize a narrative that has resisted closure in so many structural ways. Indeed, the ambiguity of the closing lines of the text is performative of psychic processes of mourning. As Loraux writes, "it is up to us, listening to Freud, to understand in all these utterances the same denial, and the confession, made without the speaker's knowledge (106). "The subject matter of a repressed image or thought can make its way into consciousness on condition that it is *denied*" (Freud, 213–214). Like Christ, Beloved is denied three times—"it was not a story to pass on"—but in the very denial there is an injunction to remember, to pass the story of Beloved on to succeeding generations. Beloved, the girl, can and must, pass away in order to ease the burden of the past borne by the community, but the emptiness left by her "passing on" is a constant reminder of her absence. Unlike the death of Christ, the passing of Beloved is not redemptive.[9] Her sacrifice does allow for the formation of community between women, both black and white, but such community, predicated on the sister's disappearance, is undeniably melancholic. The sacrifice of Beloved and the trauma that she stands for emblematizes the price of sisterhood in Reconstruction America.

Works Cited

Benjamin, Walter, "Theses on the Philosophy of History" in *Illuminations: Essays and Reflections* (Pimlico, 1999): 245–255.
Berlant, Lauren. "The Subject of True Feeling: Pain, Privacy and Politics" in *Cultural Studies and Political Theory*, Jodi Dean (ed.) (Ithaca: Cornell UP, 2000), 42–62.
—. *The Female Complaint: The Unfinished Business of Sentimentality in American Culture*. Durham: Duke UP, 2008. Print.

[9] On redemption and sisterhood at the conclusion of *Beloved* see Connie R. Schomburg's reading of Denver as fortuitously learning self-sufficiency from Beloved's overwhelming and vengeful love. For Schomberg, had Beloved not returned to elicit compensation from her mother and sister, Denver would never have approached, or learned to rely on the women of the community. Yet in insisting unequivocally upon the wholeness of the community following the exorcism of Beloved, and celebrating the "unhampered-by-the-grave bond" shared by Denver and her sister, Schomberg fails adequately to account for the ongoing guilt, pain and loss which infuse the ending of the novel. "To Survive Whole, To Save the Self," 156.

Child, Lydia Maria, "Introduction by the Editor" to Harriet Jacobs, *Incidents in the Life of a Slave Girl*. New York: Barnes and Noble, 2005). Print.

Dillon, Elizabeth Maddock. *The Gender of Freedom: Fictions of Liberalism and the Literary Public Sphere*. Stanford: Stanford UP, 2004. Print.

Emmett, Hilary, "The Maternal Contract in *Beloved* and *Medea*," in Anne Simon & Heike Bartel (eds), *Unbinding Medea: Interdisciplinary Approaches to a Classical Myth from Antiquity to the 21st Century*, (Oxford: Legenda Press, 2010): 248–260.

Freud, Sigmund. *General Psychological Theory*. Philip Rieff (ed.). New York: Macmillan, 1963. Print.

Goldsby, Jacqueline. "'I disguised my hand': Writing Versions of the Truth in Harriet Jacobs's *Incidents in the Life of a Slave Girl*, and John Jacobs's, 'A True Tale of Slavery'" in Deborah M. Garfield and Rafia Zafar (eds), *Harriet Jacobs and* Incidents in the Life of a Slave Girl: *New Critical Essays* (Cambridge and New York: Cambridge UP, 1996): 11–43.

Hartman, Saidiyah. *Scenes of Subjection: Terror, Slavery, and Self-Making in Nineteenth-Century America*. Oxford and New York: Oxford UP, 1997. Print.

Henderson, Mae G. "Toni Morrison's Beloved: Re-Membering the Body as Historical Text" in Hortense J. Spillers, ed., *Comparative American Identities: Race, Sex and Nationality in the Modern Text* (New York and London: Routledge, 1991): 62–86.

hooks, bell. *Ain't I a Woman: Black Women and Feminism*. London: Pluto, 1982. Print.

—."Sisterhood: Political Solidarity Between Women" in Anne McClintock et al., *Dangerous Liaisons: Gender, Nation, and Postcolonial Perspectives* (Minneapolis: U of Minnesota P, 1997): 396–411.

Loraux, Nicole, *Mothers in Mourning: With the Essay "Of Amnesty and its Opposite."* Ithaca: Cornell UP, 1999. Print.

Morrison, Toni. *Beloved*. New York: Knopf, 1987. Print.

—. "The Site of Memory" in William Zinsser (ed.) *Inventing the Truth: The Art and Craft of Memoir* 2nd edn (Boston: Houghton Mifflin Co., 1995): 83–102

Moten, Fred. "Black Mo'nin," in David L. Eng and David Kazanjian (eds), *Loss: The Politics of Mourning* (Berkeley: University of California Press): 59–76.

Nelson, Dana. *National Manhood: Capitalist Citizenship and the Imagined Fraternity of White Men*. Durham: Duke UP, 1998. Print.

Rushdy, Ashraf H. A. *Neo-Slave Narratives: Studies in the Social Logic of a Cultural Form*. New York: Oxford UP, 1999. Print.

Schomburg, Connie R, "To Survive Whole, To Save the Self" in JoAnna Stephens Mink and Janet Doubler Ward, *The Significance of Sibling Relation-*

ships in Literature, (Bowling Green: Bowling Green State University Popular Press, 1992): 149–57.

Stanley, Sandra Kumamoto, ed. *Other Sisterhoods: Literary Theory and U.S. Women of Color* Urbana and Chicago: University of Illinois, 1998. Print.

Stanton, Elizabeth Cady, Susan B. Anthony, and Matilda Jocelyn George, eds. *History of Woman Suffrage.* New York: Fowler and Wells, 1889. Print.

After Eden: Constructs of Home, House, and Racial Difference in Toni Morrison's *A Mercy*

Tuire Valkeakari

> I prefer to think of a-world-in-which-race-does-*not*-matter as something other than a theme park, or a failed and always-failing dream, or as the father's house of many rooms. I am thinking of it as home. "Home" seems a suitable term because, first, it lets me make a radical distinction between the metaphor of house and the metaphor of home and helps me clarify my thoughts on racial construction. Second, the term domesticates the racial project, moves the job of unmattering race away from pathetic yearning and futile desire; away from an impossible future or an irretrievable and probably nonexistent Eden to a manageable, doable, modern human activity. (Morrison, "Home" 3–4)

Rosemary Marangoly George opens her 1996 monograph, *The Politics of Home: Postcolonial Relocations and Twentieth-Century Fiction*, by observing that "over the course of the last hundred or so years, the concept of home (and of home-country) has been re-rooted and re-routed in fiction written in English by colonizers, the colonized, newly independent peoples and immigrants" (1). George's play with "roots" and "routes" echoes James Clifford's and Paul Gilroy's theorizations of diaspora, including the latter's reflections on the African diaspora in *The Black Atlantic: Modernity and Double Consciousness* (1993). Indeed, in addition to the populations mentioned by George, descendants of African slaves in North America form yet another group that has produced a significant number of anglophone novelists who are preoccupied with notions of home—among them, of course, Toni Morrison.

The title of Morrison's 2012 novel, *Home*, hardly came as a surprise to the readers familiar with her oeuvre because she has written about "home" throughout her career—that is, about domiciles and families, as well as about places of belonging in a more abstract and geopolitical sense. For example, the opening of her debut novel, *The Bluest Eye*—resonating with George's thought-provoking argument that "All fiction is homesickness" (1)—poignantly alludes to an "ideal" white middle-class home featured in a Dick and Jane primer, thereby setting the stage for young Pecola Breedlove's natural but profoundly frustrated desire to belong in her environment, domestic and beyond. In *Song of Solomon*, Milkman Dead broadens his northern, middle-class understanding of "home" (a concept that he has previously identified with his father's house, which is beautiful and immaculately kept, but virtually void of life) as he explores his family's African-derived roots in the South and, in the process, develops a new, existentially meaningful relationship to his black heritage. In *Jazz*, two southern orphans who marry and establish a home in early-twentieth-century Harlem gradually lose their shared domestic happiness, but eventually will it into being again, leaving the narrator envying the grounded everyday love that the reconciled spouses live out in their modest urban apartment. In *Paradise*, the two competing designs of "paradise" epitomized by Ruby and the Convent ultimately represent rival notions of community, group identity, belonging, and home. Because the idea of "home" in one way or another plays a pivotal part in all novels that Morrison has published to date, more examples could easily be added to these few, rather randomly selected vignettes.

Against this backdrop, it is not surprising that constructs of home,[1] as well as a profound desire to belong, figure prominently in *A Mercy*, too (as does journeying, as befits the importance, emphasized by George, of the dual theme of homesickness and movement/migration in much post-nineteenth-century anglophone fiction).[2] The present action of *A Mercy*, set in 1690, takes place on the Anglo-Dutch settler Jacob Vaark's small farm

---

[1] Although "constructs of home" is a relatively common phrase, I would like to acknowledge that my choice of it as a key concept in this article has been especially inspired by the title of Claudia Drieling's *Constructs of "Home" in Gloria Naylor's Quartet*; see also George's (11) use of the same term.

[2] While my topic resonates with the title of Anissa Wardi's "The Politics of 'Home' in *A Mercy*," Wardi is particularly interested in how the African diaspora is "represented materially as land and water" (23) in this novel. In her reading, these two elements are "embodied in Florens and Sorrow" (23), who "together [...] map a biophysical environment inflected with African diasporic history" (23). I, in turn, structure my analysis on concepts and tropes drawn from Morrison's "Home," as explained below. Also, I focus less on Morrison's representation of the African diaspora in *A Mercy* than Wardi does, because she and others have already discussed this pivotal aspect of the novel at length.

"far up north" (148) in the Province of New York—more specifically, in what is now upstate New York.[3] His homestead, a microcosm of early Atlantic America, functions as the site of the short-lived family/community formation of a handful of newcomers from various ethnoracial backgrounds to this northern region. Morrison uses her familiar cyclical style, which allows the story of each character to unfold gradually, to depict the literal and figurative journeys of Jacob, an inexperienced farmer who eventually tires of struggling with the unyielding land and responds to the siren call of the Caribbean sugar and rum trade, thus becoming a beneficiary of the Atlantic slave trade; his English wife, Rebekka, a late-seventeenth-century "mail-order bride" (Jennings 646; Wardi 23); Lina, a displaced Native American survivor, whose home village French soldiers burned down after a European-originated infectious disease had killed most of the villagers; Sorrow, a sexually and emotionally abused orphan girl of indefinite ethno-racial origin,[4] who initially seems a lost cause but then proudly renames herself Complete upon discovering her ability to be a mother; and Florens, an Angolan slave woman's teenaged New World daughter in search of both romantic love and existential self-actualization. Morrison's narrative also includes characters who frequently work as visiting laborers on Jacob's property:[5] a young, handsome blacksmith—a free black man from New

[3] The farm's New York location is implied by Jacob's references (13) to "Fort Orange" (on the site of the present-day city of Albany, NY), "Wiltwyck" (now Kingston, NY), and "Nieuw Amsterdam" (now New York City, NY). Some scholars have placed Jacob's farm in Virginia; Jennings, for example, refers to "Jacob's burgeoning Virginia estate" (646), and Peterson (10) uncritically quotes her. However, Morrison's narrative depicts Willard Bond reminiscing about the time that he spent in Virginia *before* leaving the colony for the more northerly region where his new master and Jacob live (148). Justine Tally (65; 79, n17) identifies *A Mercy*'s Milton with Milton, Massachusetts—a still-existing town that was, historically, settled by Puritans in 1640. However, the Dutch history of Jacob's farm (he inherited the estate from an uncle on the paternal, Dutch side of his family; 11–12) points to a New Netherland rather than a Massachusetts settlement. Indeed, in a 2008 interview Morrison specifically mentioned that the novel's events are set in "upstate New York and down in Maryland and Virginia" ("Back Talk").
[4] For a longer discussion of Sorrow's race, see Cantiello (165, 170, 173–75).
[5] Jacob, like other Europeans, views not only his houses but also "his" land as a commodity or property that he possesses. As Lina thinks to herself, "Cut loose from the earth's soul, they [the Europeans] insisted on purchase of its soil" (54). For a discussion of colonists' and Native Americans' different understandings of property rights concerning land in early America, see Cronon, chapter 4, "Bounding the Land." As Cronon emphasizes, the colonists, who saw the land as a commodity, understood their land "purchases" from Native Americans to mean that "what was sold was [. . .] the land itself, an abstract area whose bounds in theory remained fixed no matter what the use to which it was put" (68), whereas the Native Americans thought of themselves as dealing with usufruct rights. Cronon elaborates: "What the Indians owned—or more precisely, what their villages gave

Amsterdam—who voluntarily cares for a little foundling boy at home; and Willard Bond and Scully, white indentured servants on a farm adjacent to Jacob's, who find solace in each other's arms but lack the knowledge, political power, and wherewithal to fight the terms of their unduly prolonged bondage.[6] Morrison's project of reimagining early American racial and social formations both encompasses all these characters' journeys and highlights the way in which each character envisions belonging, individual agency, family, and home.

In *A Home Elsewhere: Reading African American Classics in the Age of Obama* (2010), Robert B. Stepto identifies the topics of "how protagonists raise themselves, often without one or both parents; [. . .] how protagonists seek and find a home elsewhere; and how protagonists create personalities that can deal with the pain of abandonment" as "age-old themes in African American literature" (5). These themes permeate—indeed, saturate—*A Mercy*, starting with the importance of the trope of orphanhood (which describes the childhood of the patriarch Jacob, too, not just the lives of his underlings) in this novel.[7] Yet, Morrison's re-imaginings of "home" in her oeuvre do not only concern the private and the personal, but also the societal and the political, regardless of whether she depicts an actual domicile or envisions home as a place of belonging in a more figurative sense. In her 1997 essay "Home" (based on her talk at the "Race Matters" Conference at Princeton University in April 1994 and published in the anthology *The House That Race Built*), she examines the concepts of "race" and "home" together. Morrison opens the essay by acknowledging that neither she nor her readers have ever "lived [...] in a world in which race did not matter" (3). She refers to the notion of "a world [...] free of racial hierarchy" as "dreamscape—Edenesque, utopian" (3) and adds that "the

---

them claim to—was not the land but the things that were on the land during the various seasons of the year. It was a conception of property shared by many of the hunter-gatherer and agricultural peoples of the world, but radically different from that of the invading Europeans" (65). In addition to marginalizing the native peoples, the colonists also made their own interpretations of property rights the law of the land.

[6] While discussing *A Mercy* with NPR's Michel Martin, Morrison emphasized that most of the characters featured in this novel are "in various stages of enslavement." Indeed, Nell Irvin Painter reminds us that "before an eighteenth-century boom in the African slave trade, between one-half and two-thirds of all early white immigrants to the British colonies in the Western Hemisphere came as unfree laborers, some 300,000 to 400,000 people," and that "the *eighteenth* century created the now familiar equation that converts race to black and black to slave" (42; emphasis added). *A Mercy*, set in the late seventeenth century, reflects these historical facts.

[7] For a reading of *A Mercy* that focuses on the trope of orphanhood, see Vega-González.

race-free world has been posited as ideal, millennial, a condition possible only if accompanied by the Messiah or situated in a protected preserve—a wilderness park" (3). However, having made these disclaimers, she then, after all, goes on to exercise her powers of utopian imagination (albeit in an emphatically domestic/ated and grounded manner) by connecting the possibility of "unmattering race" (3) with the concept of "home" in the passage quoted at the beginning of this article. While scholars have previously placed "Home" in dialogue with *Paradise*,[8] this article argues that Morrison's reflections in "Home" are extremely relevant to *A Mercy* as well: the trope of Eden, constructs of home, what Morrison in "Home" calls "a radical distinction between the metaphor of house and the metaphor of home" (3), and (early) American racial formations all play significant roles in this novel.

Jacob as an American Adam

Morrison embeds the trope of Eden in *A Mercy* by casting Jacob as "a version of the American Adam" (Conner 152)[9]—an Adam whom the reader first encounters wandering in a lush Edenic paradise, a Virginian landscape (named by the English after their Virgin Queen) that he "penetrat[es]" (9) both through his mental determination and his physical force: "Penetrating it was like struggling through a dream. [. . .] Other than his own breath and tread, the world was soundless" (9–10). Morrison's language implies that Jacob—whose "tread" (10) anticipates Native American Lina's later remark about "the deathfeet of the Europes" (54)—imposes his patriarchal will and white male desire on what may seem, at first sight, a virginal landscape, with its "forests untouched since Noah, shorelines beautiful enough to bring tears, wild food for the taking" (12). However, as William Cronon points out in *Changes in the Land*, his pioneering 1983 study of early American environmental history, it may be "tempting to believe that when the Europeans arrived in the New World they confronted Virgin Land, the Forest Primeval, a wilderness which had existed for eons uninfluenced by human hands," but "nothing could be further from the truth" (12). Paraphrasing Francis Jennings, Cronon adds that "the land was less virgin than it was widowed" because Native Americans "had lived on the continent for thousands of years" (12). As fields of study, both Native American history and American environ-

---

[8] For discussions of "Home" and *Paradise* together, see e.g. Dobbs (109–110); Valkeakari (193–200).
[9] See also Stave (140).

mental history have taken giant leaps forward since 1983; however, it is appropriate to evoke Cronon's trailblazing book here because, in a 2008 interview with Christine Smallwood, Morrison singled out *Changes in the Land* as a particularly helpful study that she had read "over and over" while doing background research for *A Mercy* ("Back Talk"). Indeed, as *A Mercy* depicts Native Americans' and colonists' markedly different attitudes to their physical environment, Morrison's prose echoes Cronon's scholarship both in the Virginian/Edenic scene and in later passages, particularly in ones in which the narration is filtered through Native American Lina's consciousness.

Because Morrison sets Jacob's journey through Virginia to Maryland in the year 1682, she does not literally cast him as either the first human or the first white man wandering in Virginia's wilderness. However, at the novel's symbolic level, this scene—with its linguistic linkage of the white American Adam's presence with what Cathy Covell Waegner aptly describes as "trampl[ing] on existing cultures, landscapes, and resources" (91)—anticipates Jacob's future avarice, corruption, and fall. Sandra M. Gustafson and Gordon Hutner (245) observe that the scene's invocation not only of European colonialism but also of (pre)capitalist greed ironically resonates with the final paragraphs of F. Scott Fitzgerald's *The Great Gatsby* (1925):[10] in *Gatsby* (189), Nick Carraway's concluding reflections connect the "fresh, green breast of the new world," which amazed early Dutch sailors when they first saw what is now a New York shoreline, with the pursuit of material wealth. *A Mercy*'s equivalent of this "green breast," and of the "green light" that "Gatsby believed in" (*Gatsby* 189), is the rising sun shining through an early morning Virginia fog that Jacob perceives as "thick, hot gold" (*A Mercy* 8). Prompted by this sight of "gold," Jacob, too—like Fitzgerald's characters—mentally connects the New World's natural resources with opportunities to accumulate wealth (Gustafson and Hutner 245). The "blinding" (10) golden haze that is capable of completely obscuring the spectator's vision here signifies a (partially deceptive) promise of easy riches to be made in the New World. Although Jacob is initially relatively indifferent to the temptation of affluence, materialistic greed increasingly dominates his decision-making as the story progresses (Gustafson and Hutner 245), eventually causing him to lose sight of all other considerations and objectives in life.

Indeed, when Geneva Cobb Moore calls *A Mercy* Morrison's "demonic parody of the colonial American experience for Native Americans, black

---

[10] Conner (154–55), too, mentions this intertextual allusion.

Africans, and black Americans" (3), she aptly elaborates that "Morrison's parodic hypertext is intended to illuminate the impoverished background of the early Europeans, and, ironically, their developing avarice and ethnocentrism" (4). As befits this aspect of Morrison's narrative design, the chapter depicting Jacob's journey highlights both his growing greed and his emerging identification with white privilege by anticipating his fall (that is, his succumbing to the temptation of becoming a beneficiary of the Atlantic slave trade) in no uncertain terms: at the chapter's end, Jacob's "plan" (35) to participate in the Caribbean rum trade—a scheme that seems to him "as sweet as the sugar on which it was based"—is already "taking shape" (35). However, at its early stages the same chapter points to Jacob's *pre*lapsarian (in this context, unselfish) characteristics as well: it discloses his "pity for orphans and strays" (33); his ethical treatment of wildlife (he briefly inter-rupts his journey to rescue a trapped raccoon; 11) and of domesticated animals (he abhors cruelty to horses; 28);[11] his intense disapproval of whites' treatment of Native Americans during Bacon's rebellion (10), a sentiment strongly suggestive of an egalitarian dimension in his politics; and his equally stern dislike of the oppressive laws encouraging antiblack racism that were enacted in the same conflict's aftermath (10–11):

> By eliminating manumission, gatherings, travel and bearing arms for black people only; by granting license to any white to kill any black for any reason; by compensating owners for a slave's maiming or death, they [the "new laws authorizing chaos in defense of order"; 10] separated and protected all whites from all others forever. [. . .] In Jacob Vaark's view, these were lawless laws encouraging cruelty in exchange for common cause, if not common virtue. (10–11)

In other words, the chapter narrating the white American Adam's journey contains both pre- and postlapsarian indications—on the one hand, intimations of what seems to be Jacob's kindness and egalitarianism and, on the other hand, evidence of his quickly deepening, profoundly self-serving desire to become rich (a craving prompted by his visit to Jublio, the

---

[11] However, the narrative's early reference to Jacob's abhorrence of the maltreatment of domestic animals takes on ambivalent, Douglassian overtones when considered together with the later revelation that Jacob eventually decides to participate in the Caribbean rum trade, a form of early Atlantic capitalism dependent on slave labor. In his 1845 *Narrative* (26), Douglass criticized his first master's employer, Colonel Lloyd, for hypocrisy, because Lloyd demanded that his horses be provided with the best possible care, but at the same time kept extremely cruel overseers of slaves on his payroll. See also Peterson (14).

plantation of the Portuguese slave owner/trader D'Ortega in Maryland), regardless of the cost of the enterprise to Africans and their descendants on the Atlantic rim. At times, such pre- and postlapsarian indications overlap, as with the description of Jacob's above-mentioned, lamentably heavy tread on the land that still resembles an Edenic paradise before the Fall. When read in light of Morrison's reference to the "probably nonexistent Eden" in "Home" (4), such an overlap speaks to the difficulty of distinguishing, in any precise or meaningful way, between the white Adam's "prelapsarian" and "postlapsarian" conditions in early post-Contact America. That is, although *A Mercy* does not completely demonize Jacob (he is cast as a fallible human, not as Satan),[12] it nevertheless implies that the white American Adam *always* was a fallen Adam—even upon arrival, while enjoying the opportunity to start afresh in the New World. For this reason, Marc C. Conner's (152) comment that Morrison's Adam "brings his corruption with him" (a statement that may sound oxymoronic, because in theological contexts Adam is assumed to have originally been pure and innocent) is on the mark. Europeans arrived as colonizers and colonists, taking their right to enter and settle in the New World for granted, as long as the relevant authorities in their respective home countries/empires had permitted their emigration (and in some cases, as with stowaways, even if no such legal permission existed). As Waegner (91) and Valerie Babb (147) emphasize, *A Mercy* offers a corrective to the Pilgrim/Puritan-dominated narrative of the first decades of English settlement in America.[13] The novel reminds us that not everyone came to the New World to flee religious persecution or to participate in the life of a newly formed theocratic society; for many, migration was precipitated by much more worldly concerns. Myriad English colonists came to the New World in search of a materially better life, which was to be acquired on their (or, more generally, on the Euro-

---

[12] See my brief discussion, in the "Conclusion" below, of Tessa Roynon's comparison of Jacob to Milton's Satan.

[13] Babb aptly notes that "Morrison uses much of the language of the 'grand myth' to rewrite it, and in so doing indicts its lapses" (147). Babb's usage of "grand myth" evokes Waegner's statement (which Babb quotes verbatim) that *A Mercy* "recalls the vexed intercultural beginnings of the settlement of the New World—rather than the grand myth of a chosen people's compact with God to establish an exemplary City upon a Hill" (Waegner 91). Babb places *A Mercy* in dialogue with such American "origins narratives"—sources of "a mythohistory of American origins" (147)—as William Bradford's *Of Plymouth Plantation*, John Winthrop's "A Modell of Christian Charity" (which Waegner ironically references above), Ralph A. Hamor's *A True Discourse of the Present Estate of Virginia*, and John Smith's *A Map of Virginia*.

peans') terms. Those terms had disastrous consequences for Native Americans, as well as for first-generation African arrivals and their descendants.

In the Virginian/Edenic scene, the American Adam's discovery of "an old Lenape trail" (10) serves as an early indicator that the seemingly "virginal" terrain on which he treads had, in the past, had an intimate and well-functioning relationship with local tribes, who had lived off the land without exploiting it. In the same scene, Jacob also reflects on the catastrophic consequences of Bacon's rebellion for the region's natives, as noted above—"the slaughter of opposing tribes and running the Carolinas off their land" (10). In the novel in its entirety, however, it is Lina who is the most visible embodiment of the Native Americans experiencing marginalization, displacement, and even extermination in the novel's present. By 1682–1690, King Philip's or Metacom's War (the 1675–76 watershed event in early American conflicts over land between Native Americans and European settlers in the Northeast) has already taken place and set the course for a future of white dominion. As Lina's internal monologue reveals, "Her people had built sheltering cities for a thousand years and [...] might have built them for a thousand more" (54), but "the Europes neither fled nor died out. [...] [L]ike all orphans they were insatiable" (54). Lina's perspective on Atlantic America—together with "Milton" (112) as the designation of where the Vaarks live[14] (a name that unmistakably suggests, for the reader, an irretrievable Eden)—emphasizes that any alleged "paradise," if it ever existed, has already been irrevocably lost:[15] the white American Adam's arrival/fall has resulted in a change that cannot be undone.

Jacob's Three Houses

As befits Lina's role as a foil to the worldview of white colonists, much of the novel's most explicit criticism of the fallen Jacob's avarice is focalized through her consciousness. As Lina's retrospective reflections on Jacob's three houses reveal, his eventual choice to embrace materialism—an option made possible by his participation, direct or indirect, in the Atlantic slave trade—makes him prioritize a "house," or a grand mansion, over a "home"

---

[14] A Mercy does not clarify whether "Milton" refers to Jacob's demesne or to the "hamlet founded by Separatists" (33) that is located some seven miles from his farm. Some scholars, therefore, treat Milton as the name of Jacob's estate, others as the name of the nearby village.

[15] For analyses of A Mercy's intertextual dialogue with Milton's Paradise Lost, see Roynon, "Her Dark Materials"; and Roynon, "Miltonic Journeys."

(to evoke again the "radical distinction" that Morrison makes between the two in "Home," 3). In 1682, when Jacob visits the D'Ortega household in Maryland, he still lives in what represents, or at least most closely resembles, a genuine "home" in the narrative—that is, the second house on his farm. The first house was, according to Lena, "weak[]" (43); Jacob's decision to replace it with a new one was therefore based on legitimate need. However, Lina recalls that "the second one was strong" (43): Jacob "tore down the first to lay wooden floors in the second with four rooms, a decent fireplace and windows with good tight shutters" (43). Because the second house was solid and warm, there was, in Lina's opinion, "no need for a third" (43). Morrison's narrative validates Lina's view by making much of the "era" of the second house coincide with a relatively stable time period in the Vaarks' life: both Jacob and Rebekka work energetically on the farm, their marriage is marked by mutual respect, and there are children in the household who supply meaning to their parents' existence (although this joy is short-lived, as all of the children die, one after the other).

However, the construction of the third house, made possible by profits from the Caribbean/Atlantic rum trade, denotes a shift in Jacob's (now, without any ambiguity, the fallen Adam's) disposition: after being seized by materialistic greed and envy at Jublio (27), Jacob goes from being content with a solid home to desiring a grandiose house that, on the narrative's symbolic level, epitomizes an insatiable ambition to own more, that is, to possess and display for the mere sake of possessing and displaying. In Lina's words, "at the very moment when there were no children to occupy or inherit it, he meant to build another, bigger, double-storied, fenced and gated like the one he saw on his travels" (43). The mansion that Jacob builds may be a "father's house of many rooms" (to evoke Morrison's ironic riff on a famous New Testament phrase in "Home," 3), but because the father's children are dead, the construction project is both unnecessary and wasteful. Given Lina's intimate relationship with nature and the land, she is particularly offended by Jacob's decision to fell as many as fifty trees to build his third house: "Killing trees in that number, without asking their permission, of course his efforts would stir up malfortune" (44)—an ominous anticipation proven correct by Jacob's death during the final stage of the project.

What makes the trope of the white Adam's fall from grace all the more ironic and tragic in the narrative is that, prior to his 1682 visit to Jublio, Jacob had always thought of the use of slave labor as a "degraded business" (31). At Jublio, he was emotionally and physically "nauseated" (22) by the overt presence of slavery in the D'Ortega household. However, his triumphant encounter, in the role of creditor, with the financially troubled slave trader reminded Jacob, stirring his greed, that in the New World the only thing separating him, a lowly farmer with humble origins, from "rich gentry" (27), such as the D'Ortegas, was material wealth; in America, no aristocratic family lineage was required for upward mobility. Later that evening, Jacob was subjected to enthusiastic tavern talk about the "beneficial effects" (29) of the Caribbean rum trade, a form of early Atlantic capitalism[16] that was supposedly easy to learn, master, and reap quick profits from. His decision to "look into it" (32) signals his fall. However, unlike D'Ortega, Jacob was determined to keep the evil of slavery out of his domestic sphere. Like English absentee owners, whose slaves toiled on remote Caribbean sugar islands out of sight, he, too, wanted his domestic life to be based far away from the growing, cutting, and cooking of sugar cane—the work done by slaves. The geographical distance between Milton and any sugar island facilitated the mental compartmentalization that helped him to justify the enterprise to himself: "There was a profound difference between the intimacy of slave bodies at Jublio and a remote labor force in Barbados. Right? Right, he thought" (35).[17] That same night, while washing his hands after a day that had included an encounter with an injured, bleeding raccoon (11), he—in a brief but chilling scene—at the same time metaphorically washed away "the faint trace of coon's blood" (35), that is, any reminder of black slaves' blood (given the use of "coon" as a racial slur).

However, despite Jacob's hypocritical attempt to wash his hands of slavery, or to wash away his guilt for benefiting from the use of slave labor, his "fall" signifies participation in a profoundly evil venture, as the iron snakes on the gate of his third house affirm for the reader. A Mercy is heavily laden with biblical, Miltonic, and other familiar symbolism resonant with early modern thought. Accordingly, the "divine punishment" that Jacob receives for his "sins" is also one of epic (or, in this case, dramatic—namely, Shakespearean) proportions, literally amounting to "plague on both his houses," to paraphrase Mercutio's famous line in Romeo and Juliet

---

[16] As for whether the use of the term "capitalism" is appropriate in this seventeenth-century context, see, for example, Joyce Appleby's remark that "nowhere is the profit-maximizing imperative of capitalism more in evidence than in the sugar sweep in Europe's New World colonies" (127). Appleby views seventeenth-century England as the cradle of the developments that led to the rise of modern capitalism (13–15).

[17] Wardi (31) and Anderson (133–34) also highlight the importance of this passage for the novel as a whole.

(III.i.95). As Jacob comes down with a fatal case of "pox" (37)—that is, smallpox (132)—his fallen condition is evident in his tragic inability to think about anything but his new possession, which now "possesses" him: instead of passing away with dignity in the building that has been home to him and his family for years, the dying patriarch insists on being carried into his new, almost complete mansion. This desire, an indication of Jacob having completely surrendered to materialism, reveals that his effort to keep the dark side of his business ventures from interfering with his domestic sphere has failed miserably: his participation in early Atlantic capitalism has profoundly changed *him*. Blinded by the Atlantic rim's "golden fog," he has no longer focused his energies and efforts on the family/community formation at "home" but, instead, on the construction of the "house" (to refer, again, back to Morrison's home/house distinction)—and the latter is the only thing that matters to him in his final hour. In a nightmarish, Gothic scene, which the reader can only access through the memories of the female characters, Rebekka, Lina, Florens, and Sorrow obediently carry the expiring, infectious patient from his "home" to his "house." At any imaginable symbolic/spiritual level, this is a movement in the wrong direction. Indeed, Lina, catching a glimpse of the iron snakes at the top of the "sinister gate" (51) as the barely breathing Jacob is being dragged inside, aptly feels "as though she were entering the world of the damned" (51).

"Race" and Racial Formations in A Mercy

Before Jacob's passing, Rebekka, Lina, Florens, and Sorrow's co-existence in his second house and on his farm in many ways reflects the fluid character of early Atlantic American racial arrangements, rather than representing "the house that race built." True, the four women's social roles are, to a degree, governed by early American society's notions of slavery and servitude, because each of the three women of color occupies a position on the spectrum of human bondage/servitude, with Rebekka as her mistress. Yet, the interactions among the four women contain a certain amount of elasticity as well, rather than being based on a completely rigid, racially determined script. For example, Lina (the "young female already in charge" when Rebekka first arrives on the farm; 53) and Rebekka ("the new wife" and, from Lina's point of view, an "awkward Europe girl"; 53) quickly overcome their initial mutual mistrust and become allies in running the household: "The animosity, utterly useless in the wild, died in the womb. [...] The fraudulent competition was worth nothing on land that demanding" (53). The two realize that, as Mina Karavanta notes, "they could survive only by learning to live and share with each other" (733). The narrative, in fact, here transcends both the mistress-slave/servant dialectic and the discourse of mutual dependence by suggesting that, at least in Lina's view, she and Rebekka "became friends" (53). Rebekka gradually forges an emotional bond with Florens as well, eventually feeling "a lot of affection for her" (96), even though as a grieving mother she at first takes umbrage at her husband's assumption that bringing home a girl of their deceased daughter's age would be a consolation (96).

In other words, the multiethnic social world of the Atlantic America that Morrison depicts is still at a very early stage of its formation—and, particularly in fairly isolated domestic units, such as Jacob's farm, this state of flux facilitates various homegrown social arrangements, including ones relatively indifferent to the emergent idea of "race." (By contrast, in the close-knit Puritan community that Florens passes through during her "errand" [4] into the "wilderness" [5],[18] the whites' shared social perception of "blackness" is much more clearly—and inimically—defined.)[19] It is true that the characters inhabiting A Mercy's world are, as Jessica Wells Cantiello observes, "all raced" (167). However, it is also true, as Cantiello adds, that "what these identities mean in 1690 is different from what they would mean in 1850 or in 2008 [the year that saw the presidential election of Barack Obama for 2009–2012]" (167). In a 2008 NPR interview with Lynn Neary, Morrison said that in A Mercy she had wanted to "separate race from slavery" by writing about an America that was still "fluid, ad hoc." The novel indeed demonstrates, throughout, Morrison's powerful awareness not only of the social constructedness of race, but also of the late seventeenth century as a cusp era with regard to racial formations in America: on the one hand, notions of racial difference had not yet ossified into a hard-and-fast pseudoscientific ideology "devised to rationalize European attitudes and treatment of the conquered and enslaved peoples" (to quote from the American Anthropological Association's 1998 Statement on "Race"); on the

---

[18] While Morrison here demonstrates familiarity with the terminology that Perry Miller famously cultivated in Errand into the Wilderness (1964) and his other works, it is certainly true, as Gustafson and Hutner observe, that A Mercy's "colonial period draws richly from recent historical and literary historical scholarship" (246; emphasis added), rather than narrowly focusing on the Puritans and their mindset (247).

[19] The only individuals who show kindness to Florens in the Puritan village are two females who are themselves outcasts in the community—namely, Widow Ealing and her daughter; the latter has amblyopia (or "lazy eye") and is therefore suspected of practicing witchcraft. For a reading that discusses A Mercy together with the Salem witchcraft trials, see Bross.

other, the gradual hardening of racial attitudes had already begun.[20] Both of these aspects of racialization in late-seventeenth-century America are present in *A Mercy*.[21]

Before Jacob dies, in the "era" of his second house all the four women living on his farm participate in the formation of a shared "home," both literally and in the more metaphorical, Morrisonian sense of participating in "the job of unmattering race" through "a manageable, doable, modern human activity" (Morrison, "Home" 3–4), however incomplete and flawed this process may be. After Jacob's demise, however, the tiny women's community begins to fall apart, largely because of the era's rigid gender roles: the New World being very little, if any, less patriarchal than the Old, the women's group cannot exist as an independent unit once the male head of the household is gone. During Rebekka's struggle with smallpox, Lina's musings on her own, Sorrow, and Florens's shared predicament speak to the consequences of the era's gender arrangement for women and girls, especially for those in bondage or servitude:[22]

> Don't die, Miss. Don't. Herself, Sorrow, a newborn and maybe Florens—three unmastered women and an infant out here, alone, belonging to no one, became wild game for anyone. None of them could inherit; none was attached to a church or recorded in its books. Female and illegal, they would be interlopers, squatters, if they stayed on after Mistress died, subject to purchase, hire, assault, abduction, exile. (58)

The women's vulnerability also arises from their lack of connection to an outside community— some "encircling outside thing," as Lena puts it (58). Uninterested in religion and piety, Jacob and Rebekka were never active as a couple in the communal life of the local European settlers, a tight-knit

---

[20] In articulating its position on how the modern notion of "race" came into being, the American Anthropological Association places a strong emphasis on the "colonial situation": "Today scholars in many fields argue that 'race' as it is understood in the United States of America was a social mechanism invented during the 18th century to refer to those populations brought together in colonial America: the English and other European settlers, the conquered Indian peoples, and those peoples of Africa brought in to provide slave labor. [...] Thus 'race' was a mode of classification linked specifically to peoples in the colonial situation. [...] As they were constructing US society, leaders among European-Americans fabricated the cultural/behavioral characteristics associated with each 'race,' linking superior traits with Europeans and negative and inferior ones to blacks and Indians" ("Statement on 'Race'"). For an overview of the rise of the idea of race in colonial Virginia, see Roediger, *How Race Survived*, chapter 1.
[21] See also Waegner (92).
[22] See also Gallego-Durán (104).

Separatist group (whose members Morrison variously calls "Anabaptists" [e.g. 44, 97] and "Baptists" [e.g. 56, 57, 89], sometimes even using both design-nations on the same page [98]). During Rebekka's illness, however, Lina realizes that the Vaarks' seemingly self-sufficient isolation had, in fact, jeopardized the future of the farm's women, who cannot survive in the wilderness by themselves: "Lina had relished her place in this small, tight family, but now saw its folly. [. . .] Their [Jacob and Rebekka's] drift away from others produced a selfish privacy and they had lost the refuge and the consolation of a clan" (58). Rebekka arrives at the same conclusion. After recovering from her illness, she turns to the locals for help. In exchange for the sense of safety, security, and belonging that the Separatist community offers her, she joylessly accepts their religious beliefs (153). The narrative also implies that she will remarry soon, in order to be able to keep the farm (145).

The disintegration of the women's community has different conse-quences for Rebekka than it does for the women of color. Being white, Rebekka is able to save herself, although the era's gender norms and the realities of frontier life mean that she must accept dependence on a male provider, or at least on the local community. Scully's musings, similarly, reflect a burgeoning understanding of what the title of David R. Roediger's 1991 book, a groundbreaking work in whiteness studies, famously calls "the wages of whiteness": Morrison's indentured servant, a white male, sees a way forward and envisions an increased mobility and independence for himself in the future (154). Lina, by contrast, is becoming much more of an Other in the Vaark household than she had been before Jacob's death. Rebekka, whose newly discovered religion requires her to eradicate any "savage" characteristics from Lina, Sorrow, and Florens's lives, now firmly resumes her role as a mistress (rather than being a "friend") and resorts to harsh educational and disciplinary measures (155). Florens's situation is the most difficult: even as she is writing her self-discovery on the floor and walls of a room in the late Jacob's mansion (a pivotal aspect of the narrative, frequently discussed in scholarship),[23] she is, in fact, for sale (155; an equally crucial aspect of the narrative, yet one often ignored by scholars).[24] As an act of rebellion and resistance, Florens plans to burn the grandiose house down (161)—possibly with help from Lina (161), who once saw whites turn her home village into ash. While at the novel's conclusion the fates of the three

---

[23] See, for example, Anderson (141–44); Christiansë (188, 193–94); Conner (163–65); Karavanta (727–29, 735–36, 739); Schreiber (170); and Wardi (34).
[24] For instance, none of the analyses referenced in note 23 mentions that Florens is for sale when she writes her agency into being.

women of color resonate with each other, the ending particularly emphasizes that the same forces that made Florens's mother a diasporic individual will keep Florens, too, in a state of involuntary migrancy in the New World, rather than providing her with a home.

Conclusion

In "Miltonic Journeys in *A Mercy*" (53–55), Tessa Roynon examines the similarities that she finds between Satan in Milton's *Paradise Lost* and Jacob in *A Mercy*. In this article, I have, in contrast—taking my cue from *A Mercy*'s passages that explicitly compare Jacob to Adam (58; 98)—discussed Jacob as an "American Adam," rather than as a biblical or Miltonic Satan figure. While R.W.B. Lewis's 1955 classic highlighted the important role of the trope of the American Adam in American Studies discourse, in 1964 Leo Marx famously put "the machine in the garden" in order to critique the potential of the American pastoral ideal to serve "a reactionary or false ideology" and to "mask the real problems of an industrial civilization" (Marx 7).[25] Morrison, in turn, puts race, in addition to social class, in the garden: she places the trope of the American Adam in dialogue with race, racialization, and racism and, in so doing, urges us to examine the role that racial formations played in American social relations even prior to the United States' nationhood. My secular "Adamic" approach has, in other words, highlighted Morrison's emphasis that racialization (which on American soil quickly ossified into pseudo-scientific racism) became pervasive in the New World as a result of *human* actions, not by virtue of any supernatural intervention, divine decree, or a "natural" order of things. It logically follows from this emphasis that the fight against racism and discrimination also requires human activity—political, legal, and cultural.

Finally, critics have, correctly, identified resonances between *A Mercy* and Morrison's 1987 masterpiece, *Beloved*, such as the motif of a slave mother harming or abandoning her daughter in order to protect the child from an even greater evil under the twisted circumstances of slavery. At the end of *Beloved*, the allegedly exorcised ghost/character Beloved—a haunting re-incarnation of enslavement—still roams the woods, pregnant with a past that may, in some form, be born again in the future. Indeed, even today, more than a quarter of a century after its publication, *Beloved* still reminds us that the legacy of slavery is present in American life in ways that have not

---

[25] For a brief but useful overview of the late-twentieth-century debate over the notion of the American self as an Adamic self, see Whalen-Bridge (304–306).

been successfully worked through. *A Mercy* delivers a message that is in keeping with that of *Beloved*, but with a particular focus on the constructedness of "race": Morrison's ninth novel emphasizes that the idea of "race" is a consequence of the American Adam's "fallen" condition (that is, of materialistic greed and its social and political applications from the early modern era onwards), not a category derived from any allegedly neutral "nature." It is a well-known fact in current America that the election of Barack Obama as President did not, in itself, magically transform the United States into a post-racial society; the structural effects of racism are still powerfully present today. *A Mercy,* published in the same month that saw Mr. Obama's election to the presidency,[26] challenges us to reflect long and hard on how we can make "the job of unmattering race" into "a manageable, doable, modern human activity" (Morrison, "Home" 3–4) and how we can participate in such an activity both locally and globally.

Works Cited

American Anthropological Association. "Statement on 'Race.'" 17 May, 1998. Web. 9 Sept. 2013. <http://www.aaanet.org/stmts/racepp.htm>.

Anderson, Melanie R. *Spectrality in the Novels of Toni Morrison*. Knoxville: U of Tennessee P, 2013. Print.

Appleby, Joyce. *The Relentless Revolution: A History of Capitalism*. New York: Norton, 2010. Print.

Babb, Valerie. "*E Pluribus Unum?* The American Origins Narrative Toni Morrison's *A Mercy.*" *MELUS* 36.2 (2011): 147–64. *Project Muse*. Web. 9 Sept. 2013.

Bross, Kristina. "Florens in Salem." *Early American Literature* 48.1 (2013): 183–88. *Project Muse*. Web. 9 Sept. 2013.

Cantiello, Jessica Wells. "From Pre-Racial to Post-Racial?: Reading and Reviewing *A Mercy* in the Age of Obama." *MELUS* 36.2 (2011): 165–83. *Project Muse*. Web. 9 Sept. 2013.

Christiansë, Yvette. *Toni Morrison: An Ethical Poetics*. New York: Fordham UP, 2013. Print.

[26] For an article-length discussion of the terms "pre-racial" and "post-racial" in the context of the 2008 U.S. presidential election and the publication of *A Mercy*, see Cantiello.

Conner, Marc C. "'What Lay Beneath the Names': The Language and Land-scapes of *A Mercy*." *Toni Morrison: Paradise, Love, A Mercy*. Ed. Lucille P. Fultz. London: Bloomsbury, 2013. 147–65. Print.

Cronon, William. *Changes in the Land: Indians, Colonists, and the Ecology of New England*. 1983. Rev. ed. New York: Hill and Wang, 2003. Print.

Dobbs, Cynthia. Diasporic Designs of House, Home, and Haven in Toni Morri-son's *Paradise*. *MELUS: Multi-Ethnic Literature of the U.S.* 36.2 (2011): 109–26. *Project Muse*. Web. 9 Sept. 2013.

Douglass, Frederick. *Narrative of the Life of Frederick Douglass, an American Slave. Written by Himself*. 1845. Douglass, *Autobiographies*. Ed. Henry Louis Gates, Jr. New York: Lib. of Amer., Coll. Ed., 1996. 1–102. Print.

Drieling, Claudia. *Constructs of "Home" in Gloria Naylor's Quartet*. Würzburg, Germany: Königshausen & Neumann, 2011. Print.

Fitzgerald, F. Scott. *The Great Gatsby*. 1925. New York: Simon and Schuster, 1995. Print.

Gallego-Durán, Mar. "'Nobody Teaches You To Be a Woman': Female Identity, Community and Motherhood in Toni Morrison's *A Mercy*." Stave and Tal-ly 103–18.

George, Rosemary Marangoly. *The Politics of Home: Postcolonial Relocations and Twentieth-Century Fiction*. Cambridge, UK: Cambridge UP, 1996. Print.

Gilroy, Paul. *The Black Atlantic: Modernity and Double Consciousness*. 1993. Cambridge, MA: Harvard UP, 1999. Print.

Gustafson, Sandra M., and Gordon Hutner. "Projecting Early American Liter-ary Studies." *American Literary History* 22.2 (2010): 245–49. *Project Muse*. Web. 9 Sept. 2013.

Jennings, La Vinia Delois. "*A Mercy*: Toni Morrison Plots the Formation of Racial Slavery in Seventeenth-Century America." *Callaloo* 32.2 (2009): 645–49. *Project Muse*. Web. 9 Sept. 2013.

Karavanta, Mina. "Toni Morrison's *A Mercy* and the Counterwriting of Nega-tive Communities: A Postnational Novel." *Modern Fiction Studies* 58.4 (2012): 723–46. *Project Muse*. Web. 9 Sept. 2013.

Lewis, R.W.B. *The American Adam: Innocence, Tragedy and Tradition in the Nineteenth Century*. Chicago: U of Chicago P, 1955. Print.

Marx, Leo. *The Machine in the Garden: Technology and the Pastoral Ideal in America*. New York: Oxford UP, 1964. Print.

Miller, Perry. *Errand into the Wilderness*. Cambridge, MA: Belknap P of Har-vard UP, 1964. Print.

Moore, Geneva Cobb. "A Demonic Parody: Toni Morrison's *A Mercy*." *The Southern Literary Journal* 44.1 (2011): 1–18. *Project Muse*. Web. 9 Sept. 2013.

Morrison, Toni. "Back Talk: Toni Morrison." Interview by Christine Smallwood. *Nation*. Nation, 8 Dec. 2008. Web. 20 Aug. 2013.

—. *Beloved*. New York: Knopf, 1987. Print.

—. *The Bluest Eye*. 1970. New York: Knopf, 2000. Print.

—. "Home." *The House That Race Built: Original Essays by Toni Morrison, Angela Y. Davis, Cornel West, and Others on Black Americans and Politics in America Today*. 1997. Ed. Wahneema Lubiano. New York: Vintage, 1998. 3–12. Print.

—. *Home*. New York: Knopf, 2012. Print.

—. *Jazz*. 1992. London: Picador, 1993. Print.

—. *A Mercy*. New York: Knopf, 2008. Print.

—. *Paradise*. New York: Knopf, 1998. Print.

—. "Toni Morrison Discusses *A Mercy*." Interview by Lynn Neary. *NPR.org*. NPR, 27 Oct. 2008. Web. 1 Sept. 2013.

—. "Toni Morrison On Bondage And A Post-Racial Age." Interview by Michel Martin. *NPR.org*. NPR, 10 Dec. 2008. Web. 1 Sept. 2013.

Painter, Nell Irvin. *The History of White People*. New York: Norton, 2011. Print.

Peterson, James Braxton. "Eco-Critical Focal Points: Narrative Structure and Environmentalist Perspectives in Morrison's *A Mercy*." Stave and Tally 9–21.

Roediger, David R. *How Race Survived US History: From Settlement and Slavery to the Obama Phenomenon*. London: Verso, 2008. Print.

—. *The Wages of Whiteness: Race and the Making of the American Working Class*. London: Verso, 1991. Print.

Roynon, Tessa. "Her Dark Materials: John Milton, Toni Morrison, and Concepts of 'Dominion' in *A Mercy*." *African American Review* 44.4 (2011): 593–606. *Project Muse*. Web. 9 Sept. 2013.

—. "Miltonic Journeys in *A Mercy*." Stave and Tally 45–61.

Schreiber, Evelyn Jaffe. *Race, Trauma, and Home in the Novels of Toni Morrison*. Baton Rouge: Louisiana State UP, 2010. Print.

Shakespeare, William. "Romeo and Juliet." *The Norton Shakespeare*. Ed. Stephen Greenblatt et al. New York: Norton, 1997. 872–941. Print.

Stave, Shirley A. "Across Distances Without Recognition: Misrecognition in Toni Morrison's *A Mercy*." Stave and Tally 137–50.

Stave, Shirley A., and Justine Tally, eds. *Toni Morrison's* A Mercy: *Critical Approaches*. Newcastle upon Tyne, UK: Cambridge Scholars Publishing, 2011. Print.

Stepto, Robert B. *A Home Elsewhere: Reading African American Classics in the Age of Obama*. Cambridge, MA: Harvard UP, 2010. Print.

Tally, Justine. "Contextualizing Toni Morrison's Ninth Novel: What Mercy? Why Now?" Stave and Tally 63–84.

Valkeakari, Tuire. *Religious Idiom and the African American Novel, 1952–1998*. Gainesville: UP of Florida, 2007. Print.

Vega-González, Susana. "Orphanhood in Toni Morrison's *A Mercy*." Stave and Tally 119–135.

Waegner, Cathy Covell. "Ruthless Epic Footsteps: Shoes, Migrants, and the Settlement of the Americas in Toni Morrison's *A Mercy*." *Post-National Enquiries: Essays on Ethnic and Racial Border Crossings*. Ed. Jopi Nyman. Newcastle upon Tyne, UK: Cambridge Scholars Publishing, 2009. 91–112. Print.

Wardi, Anissa. "The Politics of 'Home' in *A Mercy*." Stave and Tally 23–41.

Whalen-Bridge, John. "The Myth of the American Adam in Late Mailer." *Connotations* 5.2–3 (1995/96): 304–21. *Literature Resource Center*. Web. 9 Sept. 2013.

Rethinking Race Matters

Aoi Mori

One longstanding element of the hierarchies characterizing American society has been race; however, an explicit definition of this concept has been elusive and ambiguous. Oppressors have manipulated the fluidity and vagueness of race-concepts to institutionalize slavery and then to perpetuate a racial hierarchy with them on top. In order to maintain this hierarchy, moreover, various tactics have been conceived, such as propaganda promoting fear of miscegenation and the "one-drop [of blood] rule," whose criteria, despite being irrational and unaccountable, were widely accepted and prevailed in American society for a long time.

Almost 150 years have passed since the abolition of slavery, and recent years have seen the election of Barack Obama, the first African-American president of the United States. Obama's political victories in 2008 and 2012 signify at least on some level the move to a post-racial era. At the beginning of his administration especially, some people wanted to believe in Obama's ability to change a racist society for the better. In reality, of course, it is premature to believe that race no longer matters. For instance, Valerie Smith points out,

> Not only is it naïve to assume that the election of an African American president would mean the end of racism when so many markers of racial inequality still exist, but the urge to cloak oneself (or the nation) in the mantle of "post-race" also betrays an eagerness, if not a desperation, to turn from the history and the current state of racial formations in the nation. (14)

Toni Morrison, who is well aware that race continues to haunt American society, has attempted to wrestle with the problems of racial formations in America throughout her literary career. In this essay, I explore how the concept of "race" is constructed in contemporary American society through an examination of the socio-historical backgrounds embedded in Morrison's works, especially, *The Bluest Eye* (1970), *A Mercy* (2009), and *Desdemona* (2011). On the basis of these works, I will examine the skillful strategy Morrison uses to deconstruct the American racial hierarchy and recover the narrative voices of people relegated to the periphery of society for reasons of race.

Coded Racism

In a 2012 interview with Emma Brockes in the *Guardian*, Morrison describes her reaction to the Obama inauguration in January 2009. She notes:

> I felt very powerfully patriotic when I went to the inauguration of Barack Obama. I felt like a kid. The marines and the flag, which I never look at—all of a sudden it looked … nice. Worthy. It only lasted a couple of hours. But I was amazed, that music that I really don't like—God Bless America is a dumb song; I mean it's not beautiful. But I really felt that, for that little moment. (Morrison and Brockes)

Morrison actually made public a letter of endorsement for Obama's candidacy in 2008,[1] so we can imagine how thrilled she was to witness him take the oath of office. Yet Morrison's participation in the optimistic post-racial discourse of the Obama era goes only so far, for she is also all too aware of the deep-rooted racism of American society and understands that Obama's victories do not mean the end of white domination. In the interview with Brockes, she mentions the Republican presidential candidate Rick Santorum's controversial remarks on Obama during the 2012 presidential campaign:

> Did you see that the other day—Rick Santorum said "the man in the Whitehouse is a government nig—uh?"

---

[1] In the letter, Morrison admires Obama as a candidate and expresses his suitability for the position of president as follows: "In thinking carefully about the strengths of the candidates, I stunned myself when I came to the following conclusion: that in addition to keen intelligence, integrity and a rare authenticity, you exhibit something that has nothing to do with age, experience, race or gender and something I don't see in other candidates. That something is a creative imagination which coupled with brilliance equals wisdom." ("Toni Morrison's Letter to Barack Obama," *New York Observer*, January 28, 2008)

> Yes, he says he misspoke. Morrison bursts out laughing. "He said he
> didn't say that! They used to say 'government nigger' when black people
> got jobs in the post office, stuff like that. And that's what he was saying."
> (Morrison and Brockes)

Of course, since the Civil Rights movement of the 1960s, political correct-
ness in American society dictates that people should not overtly express
racist comments; instead, those who hold racist views often use coded
words for disguise, and such views might occasionally reveal themselves un-
consciously.

In fact, it is immensely difficult to eliminate racial prejudice, as Morrison
contends in her essay "Home" (1997):

> I have never lived, nor has any of us, in a world in which race did not
> matter. Such a world, one free of racial hierarchy, is usually imagined or
> described as dreamscape—Edenesque, utopian, so remote are the
> possibilities of its achievement. (3)

Although it may not be feasible to create a society free of racial hierarchy,
Morrison attempts to envision a literary world in which race does not
matter. In order to do so, she utilizes the power of language to help the
distressed and the hopeless retrieve their voice and integrity, and her
interrogation of the meaning of race is a recurring theme in her works.

The Destructive Force of Racism in The Bluest Eye

The Bluest Eye, Morrison's first novel, is the story of those who are expelled
from "home." For instance, the Breedloves, who live in a storefront apartment, not only lack a safe home but are also later "put outdoors," which is
"the real terror of life" (17), as the narrator Claudia relates. The family is
gradually dismembered and dissimilated from the community, with the
father (Cholly) sent to prison, the son (Sammy) running away, and the
mother (Pauline) and daughter (Pecola) ostracized by the community and
living in isolation. Once they are put outdoors, they are doomed to suffer a
destructive fate.

The *Dick and Jane* basal reader introduced at the beginning of the story
sets the white middle-class family as the norm in society and the reference
point for the regulation of cultural, historical, and social codes; accordingly,
it needs to be dismantled. Morrison's deconstructive intention is manifested
in her destruction of a paragraph from the *Dick and Jane* primer, gradually
breaking down its grammar and with it the symbolic order:

Here is the house. It is green and white. It has a red door. It is very pretty. Here is the family. Mother, Father, Dick, and Jane live in the green-and-white house. They are very happy. See Jane. She has a red dress. She wants to play. Who will play with Jane? [...] See mother. Mother is very nice. Mother, will you play with Jane? Mother laughs. Laugh, Mother, laugh. See Father. He is big and strong, Father, will you play with Jane? Father is smiling. Smile, Father, smile [...]

Here is the house it is green and white it has a red door it is very pretty here is the family mother father dick and jane live in the green-and-white house [...]
    Hereisthehouseitisgreenandwhiteithasareddooritisveryprettyhereist hefamily ....

(*The Bluest Eye* 3–4)

The first paragraph describes a typical white middle-class family and symbolizes the American dream of a happy family life, from which Pecola is excluded. In the second paragraph, Morrison erases the capital letters and punctuation marks. In the third paragraph, she even discards spaces between words, which makes the passage incomprehensible and meaningless. This disruption symbolizes Pecola's mental disorder and eventual failure, as she is cast out by the community in the end.

    Furthermore, the early versions of the *Dick and Jane* primer (like the one in the book) depict only white people, underscoring the absence of African-Americans in mainstream American society. As Carole Kismaric and Marvin Heiferman point out in *Growing Up with Dick and Jane* (1996), which explains the social and historic background of the primer from the 1930s to the 1960s, it was not until the sixties that an African-American family was introduced to the series. This family is described as follows:

They're here! Mike and the cute little twins, Pam and Penny. Their pretty Mother and handsome Father are here too. It's 1965, and they're the new neighbors who live next door or maybe just down the block. They make great new friends for Dick and Jane and Sally [...]. Mike is just like Dick. He's the same height, wears the same kind of clothes and runs around just as much. Mike's a leader too. He is Dick's first real friend, and more than his match at games, bike-riding and making up new things to do. Mike is great at guessing games. He organizes puppet shows, makes chalk drawings on Dick's driveway and puts on a play that makes everyone laugh. Mike's a gentleman too, neat and well-behaved. (Kismaric and Heiferman 98–99)

Although Mike's family appears to be warmly received to the neighborhood by Dick's family, we can strongly suspect that the community was racially segregated before they came. Moreover, the quotation above implies that only the African-American families who behave like white people and dress like them are welcomed to the neighborhood; that is, to the degree possible, African-American faces, culture, and history should be eradicated.

In this context, Pecola's family is much less likely than Mike's family to be accepted by the neighbors into the newly integrated community. They could hardly be less like the image of a "good" family depicted in the primer. Her alcoholic, abusive father Cholly is nothing like a gentleman, and her mother Pauline who is a domestic servant working for a wealthy white family and fantasizing that their house is hers, neglects her own family and cannot even show affection to her own daughter, whom she perceives as "ugly" (126). Pecola's parents never laugh, smile, or play with their children. What is worse, the parents find the closest thing they have to a *raison d'être* in the strife and violence of their relationship. In a sense, this couple, who are struggling every day in a racist society and deprived of their dignity and identity, might find that fighting is the only means available for them to relieve their anger, frustration, and stress. They certainly do not fit the image of the merry, fun-loving family depicted in the *Dick and Jane* primer.

In contrast to Cholly and Pauline, it is Geraldine, the mother of Pecola's classmate Junior, who manages to mostly meet white standards as she attempts to reproduce the habits of white people, suppressing any trace of African-American culture or lifestyle. She admonishes her son not to play with "niggers," because "[c]olored people were neat and quiet; niggers were dirty and loud" (87). In order to mold her son into a model "colored person," neat and well behaved, she pays careful attention to his appearance: she dresses him in white shirts and blue trousers, the same kind of clothes that Dick might wear. She pays particular attention to Junior's hair, instructing the barber to cut it as close to his scalp as possible so that his woolly curls will not show and to etch a part into his hair to approximate a white boy's hairstyle.

Geraldine's obsession with eradicating African-American traits from her family derives from her education at teachers' colleges and normal schools in the South, where the students "learn[ed] how to do the white man's work with refinement: home economics to prepare his food; teacher education to instruct black children in obedience" (83). Instilled with racialized prejudice in the guise of education, she trades her own racial identity and pride for

131

lessons in "[t]he careful development of thrift, patience, high morals, and good manners. In short, how to get rid of the funkiness. The dreadful funkiness of passion, the funkiness of nature, the funkiness of the wide range of human emotions" (83).

However, Junior, brought up by his mother to suppress his "funkiness" and "human emotions," does not receive love from her and inevitably has difficulty showing his feelings and communicating with others. Geraldine's house, which only superficially reproduces standards of white décor as dictated by the mainstream culture, lacks warmth or a feeling of welcome. Moreover, Geraldine too is subject to racism, because from the perspective of the whites she encounters there is no difference between "colored people" and "niggers." Ultimately, Geraldine has to imprison herself in her house to avoid discrimination, racism, and the destruction of her carefully con-structed fantasy. Thus, the depiction of the happy and assimilated African-American family in the *Dick and Jane* reader camouflages racial struggles that a lot of African-Americans have experienced.

The Construct of Race in A Mercy

Morrison's ninth novel, *A Mercy*, traces history back to the Colonial period (specifically, late-seventeenth-century New England) in order to re-examine the institutionalization of the American racial hierarchy. The novel embodies Morrison's attempts

> to separate racism from slavery, 'to see how it was constructed, planted deliberately in order to protect the ruling class' from the 'unpaid labour' on which their new civilisation and wealth depended." (Morrison and Rustin, "Predicting the Past")

During this era, according to Morrison, there was no explicitly racial aspect to the social hierarchy. At least until the first captured Africans were brought to Jamestown in 1619 as the labor force, white indentured laborers were exploited to cultivate the new world. Moreover, until the 1670s, Africans and their descendants who worked as indentured servants were liberated in the same way as their white counterparts when their term of service expired, and some of them even became landowners. However, in the 1670's Virginia passed a law authorizing non-Christians—Africans and their descendants and Native Americans—to be enslaved for life. Thus, race (disguised as religion or culture) was increasingly enshrined in legal and conventional ways of doing things in the seventeenth century.

In the course of her research for *A Mercy*, one of the books Morrison came across was *White Cargo*, a nonfiction book written by Don Jordan and Michael Walsh (Norris, "Toni Morrison"). The book starts with the discovery in Maryland in 2003 of the skeleton of a boy buried in trash. The authors set out to uncover the boy's identity and find that the burial can be traced back to the seventeenth century and that the boy had been a white indentured laborer who was similar to a slave both legally and in the conditions of his life. In relating this boy's history, Jordan and Walsh underline that slavery in America was not limited to black Africans and their descendants but was also inflicted on a fairly large scale on white European indentures.[2] In an interview with Michele Norris, Morrison comments that when she read the book she was surprised to learn that many white Americans are the descendants of slaves, and it is this institution that Morrison explores in *A Mercy*.

The book relates the painful histories of its central characters. Florens is a slave girl who is handed over to farmer and trader Jacob Vaark by her own mother, whom she refers to in Portuguese as "minha mãe." Vaark is an abandoned orphan himself, and his wife Rebekka is a mail-order bride shipped from England by her destitute father. Their servants—Lena, a Native American girl, and Sorrow, the mixed-blood daughter of a sea captain—are orphans. In the beginning, despite the differences in race and background, they are all vulnerable and work together to survive in the harsh environment of the colony. In fact, Jacob Vaark, raised on the street in London, lacks the practical skills to cultivate the land and the knowledge of nature to survive in the wilderness; he has to listens to Lena and a free African-American blacksmith, both of whom have the needed knowledge.

Thus, race is not at first a dividing line, a fact further emphasized by the juxtaposition of the neighbor's white European indentured servants, Willard and Scully, with the blacksmith, a free black man. Vaark commissions the blacksmith to do work for him from time to time, as he greatly appreciates his skills. Their partnership is equal despite the difference in race although the blacksmith's namelessness might foreshadow his imminent marginalization.

Jacob Vaark begins to change when he gets involved with the Caribbean rum trade. He begins to make substantial profits with little effort, and work

---

[2] For further discussion of the discovery of the skeleton and Jordan and Walsh's intention to publish a book about white indentures, see the introduction to *White Cargo*, "In the Shadow of the Myth" (11-19).

on the farm grinds to a halt as a result. Jacob isolates himself from the rest of the household, creating a hierarchical power structure. Accumulating wealth from trade, he attempts to demonstrate his power and substance and builds a huge mansion, "befitting not a farmer, not even a trader, but a squire" (88). The mansion, which he forbids the others to enter, represents the exclusive "house" of patriarchy. However, he dies before the mansion is completed. Vaark's failed attempt to build a castle indicates that his dream of maintaining a racialized house, made possible because of his profits from the slave trade, is nevertheless ultimately in vain.

Morrison's critique of Colonial-era race relations and racism is rooted in this story. She reinforces the significance of retrieving the forgotten and heretical narrative of Florens, who sneaks into Vaark's unfinished house after his death to record her life stories on the floor and the wall using the letters she secretly learned from a benevolent Catholic priest, alongside her mother. In the beginning, she addresses her stories to the blacksmith, who has rejected her love, but in the process of remembering her past she starts to recover lost ties with her mother, a slave, who was forced to hand Florens over to Vaark in exchange for a debt that her master D'Ortega could not pay Vaark back. Abandoned not only by the blacksmith but also by her own mother, Florens feels a constant sense of sorrow and loss. In recording her stories, she comes to articulate her identity, saying, "Slave. Free. I last" (161). Florens appropriates the power of written language and takes over the patriarchal house of Vaark to liberate herself, at least psychologically. Moreover, her telling evokes her mother's stories, presented in the next section, which reveal the reason why she agreed to give away her daughter to Vaark: she wanted to protect Florens from sexual abuse by the master, D'Ortega. Thus, she sent Florens away with Vaark, who saw the girl as "a human child" (166), not a sexual object as D'Ortega did. Morrison ends the novel by uniting the mother and the daughter through their juxtaposed narratives, as if they were talking to each other beyond space and time.

Questioning the Concept of Race in Desdemona

One of Morrison's latest works is a play, *Desdemona*, which was produced for the stage in Vienna in May 2011 in collaboration with director Peter Sellars and composer/actor Rokia Traoré and then published in 2012. It is a response to Shakespeare's *Othello* (1604). It is told from the perspective of Desdemona and focuses on her relationship with her childhood nursemaid, Barbary (named such because she was taken from the Barbary Coast, that is, the coastal Maghreb), who had committed suicide after a failed love affair.

The play is set in the world of death, where Desdemona resides after being strangled by Othello. Morrison places Desdemona's attachment to her nursemaid at the center of the play, relating that it is because of her love for Barbary and all the intriguing stories Barbary had told her about Africa that Desdemona fell in love with Othello; at first sight, Othello reminded her of Barbary. The scene in which Desdemona and Othello meet for the first time is recalled by Desdemona as follows:

> Bountifully fed, they began to dance—partnered, formal, predictably flirtatious. Hoping to exit the mockery, I stood and moved toward my father to ask to be excused. Among those huddled around his chair was this mass of a man. Tree tall. Glittering in metal and red wool. A commander's helmet under his arm. As I approached, he turned to let me pass. I saw a glint of brass in his eyes identical to the light in Barbary's eyes. I looked away, but not before his smile summoned my own. I don't remember what I murmured to my father to explain my approach. I was introduced to the Commander; he kissed my hand, held it and requested a dance. "By your leave, Senator Brabantio?" In accented language his voice underscored the kiss. (23)

What is noteworthy is that Othello, an African soldier, is allowed to attend a party that the Venetian nobleman Brabantio holds to find his daughter a suitable husband. Eventually Desdemona marries Othello, which means that her parents approve at least tacitly of their interracial marriage.

Consider as a counterexample the situation in Margaret Mitchell's *Gone With the Wind* (1936). It is almost impossible to imagine an African or African-descended suitor allowed to be near Scarlett O'Hara. The novel is set in Atlanta and rural Georgia during the Civil War and Reconstruction, an era in which racism was completely embedded in the culture and society; as a result, miscegenation is totally abhorred, and black people are relegated to the margins and made invisible. Morrison's scene in *Desdemona* is thus a response to more contemporary attitudes, emphasizing that the figure of the white supremacist is a product of late-modern colonialism and the Enlightenment and that previous eras such as Shakespeare's early modern England or the medieval Mediterranean that *Othello* depicts were not racialized in anything like the same way.

Furthermore, in *Desdemona*, Morrison attempts to recover the voice and presence of Africa, which have often been silenced and misrepresented by the white-dominated Western societies. The scene in which Desdemona reencounters Barbary in the world of death reveals the racial hierarchy that existed between them when they were alive: although Desdemona believes that Barbary was her best friend, the latter demurs, saying, "I was your slave" (45). In the world of death, however, Barbary subverts the power structure to recover her identity, reclaiming her own name, Sa'ran, and the history of her people, who live in a colonized land. She admonishes Desdemona for her naïve image of "Barbary":

> SA'RAN: I mean you don't even know my name. Barbary? Barbary is what you call Africa. Barbary is the geography of the foreigner, the savage. Barbary? Barbary equals the sly, vicious enemy who must be put down at any price; held down at any cost for the conquerors' pleasure. Barbary is the name of those without whom you could neither live nor prosper. (45)

Explicating her colonized status, Sa'ran reminds Desdemona that it was only because of her subjugated rank as a slave that she had served the girl and satisfied all her needs. In articulating the real nature of their former relationship, Sa'ran's voice is restored, and Desdemona listens to her while also trying to foster a nurturing sisterhood between them, as both of them are women who share the same experience of being abused by men whom they love.

Furthermore, Morrison's creation in the play of two characters who do not appear in *Othello*—Madam Brabantio, the mother of Desdemona, and Soun, the mother of Othello—also displays her intention to transcend class, racial, and even religious differences. The two women meet after their children, Desdemona and Othello, die. Despite the fact that they are enemies, as Desdemona was killed by Othello, they are also bound together as mothers, sharing the grief of losing a child. They are of different religions: Madam Brabantio is a Catholic who prays to "Mother Mary" (27), while Soun speaks to her own gods, not the almighty Christian God. Yet they transcend these differences too, by building "an altar to the spirits who are waiting to console [them]" (27). The altar they build together fills the gap between them, representing the hope that they can overcome the differences by sharing each other's pain. Their prayers will merge into one voice, recovering and asserting the presence of the subjugated.

Conclusion

With the advent of European colonialism, beginning before Shakespeare's period in the so-called Age of Exploration, from the late fifteenth century, but not achieving the status of a world-system until the eighteenth and nineteenth centuries, Western conquerors of non-Western societies imposed Christianity and institutionalized racial hierarchies, placing themselves on top of the social scale in subjugated places. In contrast, during the medieval period, it was the Islamic power that prospered in Turkey and Northern Africa and controlled much of the world. It was the establishment of global capitalism, rooted in colonialism and Western industrialism that accelerated white supremacy, resulting in the construction of a white-dominated racist hierarchy that relegated people of color to the periphery in the United States as well as in other places.

Toni Morrison has long defied the destructive legacy of these racial hierarchies and attempted to move beyond racial prejudice and stereotypes by returning to a pre-racialized time. Morrison's works generate spaces free of racism and, significantly, lay the foundations of a space where "race does not matter," in contradistinction to the exclusive, racialized house. Morrison reconstructs a new space beyond the segregating, detrimental black/white dichotomies of race and beyond differences of gender and religion as well.

Works Cited

Jordan, Don and Michael Walsh. *White Cargo: The Forgotten History of Britain's White Slaves in America*. NY: NYUP, 2007. Print.

Kismaric, Carole and Marvin Heiferman. *Growing Up with Dick and Jane: Learning and Living the American Dream*. New York: HarperCollins, 1996. Print.

Morrison, Toni. *The Bluest Eye*. 1970. New York: Plume, 1993. Print.

—. *Desdemona*. Lyrics Rokia Traoré. Foreword Peter Sellars. London: Oberon, 2012. Print.

—. "Home." *The House That Race Built*. Ed. Wahneema Lubiano. New York: Vintage, 1998. Print.

—. *A Mercy*. New York: Knopf, 2008. Print.

—. "Toni Morrison's Letter to Barack Obama." *The New York Observer*. 28 Jan 2008. Web. 1 Nov. 2013.

— and Emma Brockes. "Toni Morrison: 'I Want to Feel What I Feel. Even If It's not happiness.'" *Manchester Guardian*. 13 Apr 2012. Web. 15 July 2013.

— and Susanna Rustin. "Predicting the Past." *Manchester Guardian*. 1 Nov. 2008. Web. 3 Nov. 2013.

— and Christine Smallwood. "Back Talk: Toni Morrison." *The Nation*. 19 Nov. 2008. Web. 3 Nov. 2013.

Norris, Michele. "Toni Morrison Finds 'A Mercy' in Servitude." NPR Online. 27 Oct. 2008. Web. 3 Nov. 2013.

Smith, Valerie. *Toni Morrison: Writing the Moral Imagination*. West Sussex, UK: Wiley-Blackwell, 2012. Print.

"This house is strange":
Digging for American Memory of Trauma,
or Healing the "Social" in Toni Morrison's *Home*

Laura Castor

When asked in an interview about the inspiration for her latest novel, *Home* (2012), Toni Morrison characterizes "home" as a place where people "may or may not like you, but they are not going to hurt you."[1] In contrast, she says that "houses" in the 1950s, the period in which the novel is set, were part of a larger collective American idea: "World War II was over. People were buying houses, and everything was nice and comfortable. And I didn't think so." (Morrison Interview with Torrence Boone). Morrison thought that something underneath was being silenced, and in her novel she explores various forms of that silence.

As early as the book's epigraph, Morrison introduces, in a poem, the word "house" to complicate the "home" of her title. To a reader not yet aware of the novel's historical context, the word choice might appear to be a synonym for home. Yet in the "house" of the poem, the idea of a familiar safe haven is turned into something uncannily[2] unfamiliar: "This house is strange/ Its shadows lie./ Say, tell me, why does its lock fit my key?" (Morrison, *Home* Epigraph). The question for the reader is whether or not

---

[1] See also Morrison's longer, more evocative image of "home" in her 1997 essay: "In this new space one can imagine safety without walls, can iterate difference that is prized but unprivileged, and can conceive of a third, if you will pardon the expression, world 'already made for me, both snug and wide open, with a doorway never needing to be closed'" ("Home," 12).

[2] I refer both to "uncanny" in the English sense of seeming to have a supernatural or inexplicable, mysterious quality, and also as Gayatri Spivak uses it as the Freudian *unheimlich,* not at all homey or comfortable. Rather, it is "the entrance to the former *Heim* [home] of all human beings, to the place where each one of us lived once upon a time and in the beginning" (Sigmund Freud, "The Uncanny" 245 qtd. in Spivak 74).

there may be a difference between the "home" of the title and this or that "house."

In the novel, houses are discrete places located in towns, in states, and in countries that literally and figuratively "house" the expectations, the questions, and the struggles of the main characters to find healing from the personal and societal violence they have experienced and internalized. The ideal of "home," on the other hand, is an imaginative space more than a concrete reality. At worst, it is a childhood fantasy that is not possible in the world as it is. At best, "home" represents a tentative yet resilient possibility. It has many expressions, and is made palpable as Morrison's characters, both in their own idiosyncratic ways and together, try to find it in the social sphere, in the sense that Carolyn Forché uses "the social" in her Introduction to *Against Forgetting: Twentieth-Century Poetry of Witness* (31). For Forché, the more usual distinction between the personal and political as space for social change is problematic because on the one hand, the "political" may be too general-ized, while speaking of the "personal" is often too short-sighted, and assumes more and less individual choice than may be the case. In the "social" spaces between these poles, however, there is room for contingent but more direct action that connects the needs for personal healing with strategies that might eventually have an influence on the political realm. Whether or not political change results, real conflicts can be addressed, and perhaps worked through in the realm of the "social" (Forché 31).

Morrison's narration weaves together several interconnected social spaces, especially through the stories of the main characters, Korean War veteran Frank Money, and his younger sister Cee. Cee, her brother learns soon after his return from the war, has been subjected to abusive experi-ments by a doctor in Atlanta, Georgia, who hired her to work for him. She is teetering on a narrow ledge between life and death, and it becomes Frank's mission to help her. Cee has her own story, which includes Frank's older-brother affection and protection, but also a growing sense of inner strength as a woman who can welcome his comfort but doesn't need his protection.

Cee and Frank's personal development is influenced both directly and indirectly by the broader cultural silences of the Fifties, including the per-sonal and political fears of many Americans that perhaps the post-war world was less safe and comfortable than portrayed in the media. There was the fear of communism outside US borders in the Korean War, and the anti-communism within US borders. In *Home,* fear of communism is also inseparable from racial fears generated by the legacy of slavery in the South.

Hostility toward political and racial "others" becomes part of a single, inter-woven fabric inside various houses in the novel.

Along with the historical context of 1950s as a period of apparent prosperity following the upheavals of World War II, Morrison says that a second starting point for her novel was the "experimentation on helpless people" that took place during that decade (Morrison Interview with Torrence Boone). Among the most notorious, and the one that Morrison mentions as having directly influenced the development of *Home* was the Tuskegee Study, a government-initiated project designed to observe the progression of syphilis. From 1932 to 1972, 399 African American men with the disease, and 201 who did not have it, were unknowingly made subjects of this study. While those inflicted with syphilis were told that they were being treated for "bad blood," U.S. Public Health Service officials were consciously withholding treatment from them (*Bad* N. pag.).

Granted, the idea of America as a land of promise where anybody can arrive and enjoy the rights to "life, liberty, and the pursuit of happiness" declared in the Declaration of Independence, has been challenged by writers and activists from the time of the American Revolution.[3]

Nevertheless, the assumption of America as a land of freedom and equality for all remains alive in the popular imagination. It remains potent as unfulfilled promise for many people (such as but not limited to minority groups), including many of the writers who have spoken of its absence. Just as clearly, the idea of America rings true for conservative white men who see the ideal as a lost tradition in need of rejuvenation.

Morrison questions this popular rhetoric, and her narration expresses the various ways that the ordinary but hidden effects of war in everyday life complicate "life, liberty, and the pursuit of happiness." For Morrison, war is not the popularized "movie" where we want the friends of American liberty to win, and the bad guys to lose. Instead, she makes war and the trauma that accompanies it, familiar. Rather "war" is an idea as well as an extreme experience on one end of a continuum, where at the other end we find "home." These ideas of war and home move between the familiar and

---

[3] Throughout American literary history, imaginative writers from Nathanial Hawthorne to Mark Twain, Herman Melville, Frederick Douglass and Harriet Jacobs in the nineteenth century, to William Faulkner, W.E.B. DuBois, Zora Neale Hurston, Kurt Vonnegut, N. Scott Momaday, Leslie Marmon Silko, and numerous others in the twentieth century have pointed to the gaps between the American promise of, and the realities of freedom. Since the 1960s, intellectual historians have drawn on their insights to articulate these contradictions in what they term a "post-nationalist" approach to American studies (Noble xxiii).

unfamiliar as she locates them in various houses. In the novel, war is waged not only on a battlefield, but also in the so-called privacy of the house, which for some of the characters is as close to the ideal of "home" as they have come. To use Forché's approach, it might be said that the main characters' sense of dis-ease with the *unheimlich* atmosphere of their houses leads them to create "the social" in relationships and spaces that allow them to do the slow work of healing.

The reader's task is to keep asking questions about the apparent truths or hidden lies the characters tell as they try to make sense of themselves as whole, rather than traumatized men and women. Morrison provokes us to pay attention without flinching from their traumas, and she leads us to witness their healing. Healing for Cee and Frank relates to "home" as a temporary but safe haven where strength and a sense of agency can become real, for now and in the future. For Morrison's characters, healing honors rather than seeks to erase scars. It is represented poignantly in the image of a tree at the end of the novel: "I stood there a long while, staring at that tree/ It looked so strong/ So beautiful./ Hurt right down the middle/But alive and well" (Morrison, *Home* 147).

As readers we actively participate in her characters' healing through the multiple voices of her narrators. Through Morrison's shifts in narrative perspective, we enter imaginatively into "the social" arena where the novel's cultural work takes shape. In many parts of the text we hear Morrison as omniscient third person storyteller who confidently assumes the ability to focalize events through the shifting perspectives and priorities of characters in various places and times. We hear the narrating first person voice of Frank who, at regular intervals, seems to talk back to the third person narrator to reveal a different version of the Frank she narrates. Toward the end of the novel, Frank's first person narrator seems to change his mind about parts of his story. Although he admits to "lying" both to Morrison and the reader, and to himself, we don't know for sure whether it is only at this point that he can recognize his "lies" or whether he deliberately misled himself and us (Morrison, *Home* 133). These possibilities also suggest that some of what the third person narrator has relayed may be equally unreliable.

The interplay between multiple narrating voices (in both first and third person), and focalizing views (through the third person voice) is important because it deepens the readers' awareness about how necessary it is to question our ideas about truth, whether personal or collective—through questioning, we may build larger spaces for our own sense of "the social" both in our reading of the text, and in our worlds outside it. Truth is multiple, and no one narrator or reader holds all its expressions. Yet truths are partially shown through characters, and through the multiple sides of Frank that we see through the different narrations. In narrative terms, the reader sees more deeply and broadly into the multi-layered identities of the characters through Morrison's shifting narrative perspectives. In terms of historical identity, we see, through their eyes, the multiple truths in American culture and history differently as time progresses and we gain new knowledge about the complexities of the racial and gendered American past. For Morrison, the responsibility of art is, as Eudora Welty expressed it, paradoxically about "making reality real" (Welty 128).

Gayatri Spivak, in *Death of a Discipline* (2003), helps to bring these more complex truths into our habitual talk about race and gender differences, to concepts such as "mother, nation, god, nature" and, I would add, "home" (73). "If we imagine ourselves as planetary subjects rather than global agents," she says,

> planetary creatures rather than global entities, alterity remains un-derived from us; it is not our dialectical negation, it contains us as much as it flings us away. And thus to think of it is already to transgress, for, in spite of our forays into what we metaphorize, differently, as outer and inner space, what is above and beyond our own reach is not continuous with us as it is not, indeed, specifically discontinuous (73).

With respect to Morrison's shifting narrative perspectives, Spivak's reframing would mean that no single perspective, whether our own as readers, or one of the narrators' can offer a singular truth. Neither we, nor the narrators or characters, are pure "agents" who accurately interpret the core meaning of events. Yet neither is any one perspective untrue in a larger, dynamic planetary sphere where we participate together, but do not control. The effort to deal adequately with societal problems of race and gender, in this view, does not end with social science studies seeking representative truths for "women" or "African Americans" as groups. In narrative terms, the corollary to such analytical categories would be to rely on the God's eye perspective of a single omniscient narrator. Morrison's tapestry of various narrative perspectives is therefore central to her cultural work toward healing the traumatic effects of American race and gender oppression. For both Morrison and Spivak, the layers of difference and injustice that create "others" who are seen as less human and worthy of dignity, need to be unpacked, made unfamiliar and particular.

143

The meaning of "home" necessarily includes the ability to heal in a way that dares to remember—through imaginative power coupled with actual, visceral memory in a social sphere of time and place. For Morrison's readers, this might mean we have our own particular responses to violence of scenes such as in the opening pages:

> [...] we saw them pull a body from a wheelbarrow and throw it into a hole already waiting. One foot stuck up over the edge and quivered, as though it could get out, as though with a little effort it could break through the dirt being shoveled in. We could not see the faces of the men doing the burying, only their trousers; but we saw the edge of a spade drive the jerking foot down to join the rest of itself. When [Cee] saw that black foot with its creamy pink and mud-streaked sole being whacked into the grave, her whole body began to shake. (4)

The shaking that Cee does is a beginning of her own healing. Peter Levine, in *In an Unspoken Voice* describes shaking as one of the necessary ways that humans, as animals do, begin to absorb and release the effects of trauma in and from their bodies, thus allowing themselves to begin to heal (9). It is ironic that in the opening scene, Frank assumed that his role was to protect his little sister, but here the reader sees that it is Cee whose healing begins first.

As Cee's recovery process started with her shaking, so Frank's process begins again after the war when he loses, and then regains his ability to see color. Color disappeared when he had received his discharge papers in Fort Lawton, Washington, and the world he saw had turned to black and white. Whenever some color returns, the third person narrator tells us, he knew a break from his post-traumatic stress was near (23). A break comes "under a Northern oak, [where] the grass turned green"(24). The color green will also, at the end of the novel, be the color, a more nuanced "olive green," of the leaves of a sweet bay tree where Cee and Frank are finally able to give a proper burial to the person whose body they had seen thrown in the ditch in the opening chapter.

If we become aware of an ongoing trajectory of coming "home" that takes various shapes and colors (such as the imagery of trees and the return of color for Frank) throughout the novel, there also are other interlocking stories about houses that complicate and connect the process. An important related story is one about Frank and Lily, whom he meets and falls in love with in Chicago. Morrison narrates a story parallel to that of Frank and Cee through her story of Lily as focalizer. Spivak would understand this shift in narrative perspective as about "collectivity" that is always contingent and partial.[4] Frank's worldview cannot hold the perspective that Lily has. The narrator observes:

> Living with Frank had been glorious at first. Its breakdown was more of a stutter than a single eruption. She had begun to feel annoyance rather than alarm when she came home from work and saw him sitting on the sofa staring at the floor. One sock on, the other in his hand. (75)

The reader can imagine Frank with one bare foot, and remember that in the opening scene of the body thrown into the hole, the body part the children see is "that black foot with its creamy pink and mud-streaked sole" (4). As disjointed and disconnected as Frank seems to Lily, the reader might also recognize the connection to a larger process of coming to honor all of his experiences, including this more seemingly mundane breakdown of domestic relations.

But while Frank works through his own complicated past, Lily has a different agenda, at least according to the narrator. (We do not have the privilege of hearing her first-person story as we do Frank's). For Lily, who tries to see Frank's perspective, "underneath the pile of complaints [about Frank] lay her yearning for her own house. It infuriated Lily that he shared none of her enthusiasm for achieving that goal" (75). This yearning is not a superficial one in the context of 1950s American culture, when many more Americans were able to afford their own houses than at any time in US history (May 166). Yet what was not talked about in popular discourse was overt prejudice against non-whites. Morrison notes in her interview with Torrence Boone that Lily's experience of reading an advertisement from a realtor in a Chicago paper was taken from an actual announcement (*Restrictive Covenants Database*).

> Lily traced the lines of print with her forefinger. No part of said property hereby conveyed shall ever be used or occcupied by any Hebrew or by any person of Ethiopian, Malay or Asiatic race excepting only employees in domestic service." (73)

In spite of the racially restrictive words in the housing covenant, she continues to want to "buy that house or one like it (74). Frank, however, is

---

[4] Spivak includes an interesting discussion of "collectivity" in narrative in her reading of Virginia Woolf's *A Room of One's Own* (43-45).

not able to share her goal; nothing in his experience in Lotus, in the war, or in returning from the war, has made space for it as desirable or important. Lily, in continuing to pursue her goal of owning her own house, comes from a more empowered place than either Cee or Frank. Her story is valuable in allowing the reader to tie the various events of the novel back to Morrison's title, and back to the historical context of American expectations about prosperity during the Fifties.

The more nuanced stories of Frank and Cee's development toward wholeness is important to Morrison's large narrative vision, however, because they represent an extreme of what W.E.B. Dubois expressed as the "double consciousness" of being both American and African American that affords an ability to see underlying power differences and injustices more clearly (DuBois 12). For both Frank and Cee, empowerment is about healing as self-healing in a supportive community that brings one closer to home. In contrast, genuine healing does not happen in the houses and institutions of the medical establishment.

The medical "mastery" practiced in these houses expresses both the kinds of attitudes the US government demonstrated in experiments such as the Tuskegee Study, and also, the practices of slave masters. Like the subjects of the Tuskegee Study, neither Frank nor Cee is aware of the dangers confronting them. The reader, though, has a close-up view of Frank and Cee's unfolding experiences, and in that light, we see larger patterns of racism: We sense the violence that could have happened to Frank through the third person dialogue between Frank, travelling back to Georgia, and the minister ironically named John Locke who gives him a place to stay after he escapes from a hospital:

> "You from down the street? At that hospital?"
>
> Frank nodded while stamping his feet and trying to rub life back into his fingers.
>
> Reverend Loc4ke grunted. "Have a seat," he said, then, shaking his head, added, "You lucky, Mr. Money. They sell a lot of bodies out of there."
>
> [. . .] Well, you know, doctors need to work on the dead poor so they can help the live rich." (12)

When she begins working for the doctor in Atlanta, like Frank who is unaware of the danger just escaped as he sits on John Locke's sofa, Cee's attention moves first to the comfort of the bed where she'll be sleeping, rather than seeing other more ominous signs in that house about the doctor:

[. . .] she plopped on the bed, delighting in the thickness of the mattress. When she pulled the sheets back she giggled at its silk cover. So there, Lenore, she thought. What you sleep on in that broke-down bed you got? Remembering the thin, bumpy mattress Lenore slept on, she couldn't help herself and laughed with wild glee. (63)

Cee is unable to recognize what the third person narrator sees in the design of Dr. Beau's house. Whereas she views it is a refuge from memories of abuse and abandonment, the reader notices a subtext of anti-communism, racism, and misogyny. For example, Sarah, the domestic worker who become Cee's friend, a good one in that she later helps save her life through the letter she writes to Frank, says to Cee:

"Let me show you to your room. It's downstairs and not much, but for sleep it's as good as anything. It's got a mattress made for a queen." Downstairs was just a few feet below the front porch—more of a shallow extension of the house rather than a proper basement. Down a hall not far from the doctor's office was Cee's room, spotless, narrow, and without windows. Beyond it was a locked door leading to what Sarah said was a bomb shelter, fully stocked. She had placed Cee's shopping bag on the floor. Two nicely starched uniforms saluted from their hangers on the wall. (63)

While Cee's gaze is lured to the soft mattress, the narrator shows the reader the narrow, windowless room whose space seems designed to confine its occupant. It insures that the doctor, with his office nearby, will maintain control, not only over her workday, but over the most intimate aspects of her life. As suggested by image of the "starched uniforms salut[ing] from their hangers on the wall," Cee even sleeps under his militaristic surveillance. The ghostly presence of invisible bodies on the hangers is a haunting allusion to the lynching of blacks in the south, the practice of which we are led to believe Dr. Beau, a "heavyweight Confederate," would approve (62).

It is not likely a coincidence that the bomb shelter is next to Cee's windowless bedroom. His fear of outside Communist threats is accompanied by aggression, both active and passive, as he tries to maintain complete control over what happens in his house. This aggression means that he will drug and sterilize Cee for the sake of his work as a "scientist" (61). His control is political, racial, and gendered.

When Frank attempts to rescue Cee from the doctor, there are limits to how he can help. The difference between the comfort that he can keep giving her, and dependency that she eventually will no longer need, is crucial. Cee learns to discern this difference through the affirming power of Ethel Fordham and the community of women around her. Their healing abilities thrive on living tradition and empathy, in a social space outside, and in opposition to the medical industry (122). Their methods draw on the music of spirituals, gospel hymns, banjos, and mouth harps, bright sunshine, and knowledge of how to plant flowers that "protect vegetables from disease and predators" (117). In effect, this nonviolent, but by no means passive approach protects Cee from the predator of a doctor and the illness he caused in the name of "the value of the examinations" (122).

The techniques Ethel and the other women choose are specific to Cee's condition, and she learns to heal herself as a woman in a space apart from any man, including her brother. From the one girl who will talk to him, Frank learns that the women "believed his maleness would worsen her condition. She told him the women took turns nursing Cee and each had a different recipe for her cure. What they all agreed upon was his absence from her bedside" (119).

What the women also agree on is that Cee needs to learn to trust herself, and they help her to do so through collective wisdom they pass on to her:

> "You ain't a mule to be pulling some evil doctor's wagon."
> "You a privy or a woman?"
> "Who told you you was trash?"
> "You good enough for Jesus. That's all you need to know." (122)

Their tactics evolve, moving from words to action that refuses victimization in any form, whether personal, social, or societal:

> Now they brought their embroidery and crocheting, and finally they used Ethel Fordham's house as their quilting center. Ignoring those who preferred new, soft blankets, they practiced what they had been taught by their mothers during the period that rich people called the Depression and they called life. Surrounded by their comings and goings, listening to their talk, their songs, following their instructions, Cee had nothing to do but pay them the attention she had never given them before. (122)

Frank and Cee, then, find home together and separately. Cee's healing in the company of women brings her to a place where she can accept the comfort Frank offers without depending on him to be able to function in the world (131). In the final chapter, Cee and Frank stand together in a new social space that expresses their new, collective power: Cee's quilt—which is useful, and also symbolic of the community of women near and far away, past and present—becomes the cover for the man to whom they give an honorable burial. Frank writes "Here stands a man" (145) on the marker they make for his grave; we now know that Frank is giving himself honor as a man, too. He has become a man who can express his strength without resorting to violence. The tree's stance is also a metaphor for his own and for Cee's achievement: It is "hurt on the inside but still strong and beautiful" (147). Cee has the final word of the novel, when she says, "Come on brother, and let's go home" (147). Here she reminds the reader of what Frank yearned to accomplish from the moment he received the letter warning that she was near death—to bring her home. But now it is Cee's power as a person and woman that gives her confidence, and the care, to lead her brother home.

This home is a specific one where inhabitants are strengthened through a social space. It is both about being healed and continuing to heal the social, as a man and as a woman. It is about moving forward together with the resilience and power of tradition, and with healing communities at their backs. The *Home* of the title has energy because, not in spite of illness, oppression, and past mistakes. Home is also a quiet center, and it is a mindset large enough to hold what Spivak calls the planetary, constructed and then re-found (Spivak 73). Like the power of jazz, Morrison's *home* creates a momentum that unsettles even as it energizes, as it stays just a little ahead of the familiar beat.

Works Cited

Bad Blood: The Tuskegee Syphilis Study. Claude Moore Health Sciences Library: Historical Collections Online Exhibit. University of Virginia. 2007. http://exhibits.hsl.virginia.edu/badblood/. N. pag. 8 September 2013. Web.

DuBois, W.E.B. *The Souls of Black Folk*. Rockville, MD: Arc Manor, 2008.

Forché, Carolyn, Introduction. Forché 29–47.

Forché, Carolyn, Ed. *Against Forgetting: Twentieth-Century Poetry of Witness*. New York: Norton, 1993. Print.

Freud, Sigmund. "The Uncanny." *The Standard Edition of the Psychological Works,* tr. Alix Strachey et al. New York: Norton, 1961. Print.

Levine, Peter. *In an Unspoken Voice: How the Body Releases Trauma and Restores Goodness.* Berkeley: North Atlantic, 2010. Print.

Lubiano, Wahneema, Ed. *The House that Race Built: Original Essays by Toni Morrison, Angela Y. Davis, Cornel West, and Others on Black Americans and Politics in America Today.* New York: Vintage, 1997. Print.

May, Elaine Tyler. *Homeward Bound: American Families in the Cold War Era.* New York: Basic, 1988. Print.

Morrison, Toni. *Home.* New York: Knopf, 2012. Print.

—. "Home." Lubiano 3–12.

—. Interview with Torrence Boone. *Home Authors at Google.* 27 February 2013. http://www.youtube.com/watch?v=pBDARw5fdrg. 8 September 2013. Web.

Noble, David. *Death of a Nation: American Culture and the End of Exceptionalism.* Minneapolis: U of Minnesota P, 2002. Print.

Restrictive Covenants Database: Seattle Civil Rights and Labor History Project. http://depts.washington.edu/civilr/covenants_database.htm. N. pag. 29 August 2013. Web.

Spivak, Gayatri Chakravorty. *Death of a Discipline.* New York: Columbia UP, 2003. Print.

Welty, Eudora. "Place in Fiction." Welty 116–33.

Welty, Eudora. *The Eye of the Story: Selected Essays and Reviews.* New York: Random House, 1977.

Woolf, Virginia. *A Room of One's Own.* New York: Harper, 1989. Print.

Notes on Contributors

Lucy Buzacott is a PhD student at the University of Queensland, Australia, in the school of English, Media Studies, and Art History. Her thesis considers representations of mammy and belle figures in the novels of William Faulkner.

Laura Castor is Professor in English literature and culture studies at the University of Tromsø, where she teaches a graduate level course on Toni Morrison. She has published extensively on Native American literature, and is currently working on a project that explores how collective memory of trauma is expressed in fiction, poetry, and forms that cross genre boundaries.

Hilary Emmett is a Lecturer in the School of American Studiesat the University of East Anglia. She is the author of articles on North American and Australian literature and culture including a chapter analysing the relationship between Morrison's *Beloved* and the myth of Medea. Her articles on literary representations of race, settler colonialism and indigenous dispossession in Australia and the United States have appeared in *Westerly*, *Common-place* and in the forthcoming *Oxford Handbook to Charles Brockden Brown*.

Giulia Grillo Mikrut received a BA and a MA from Stockholm University. Since 2009 she has been a PhD candidate in the School of English, Media Studies, and Art History at the University of Queensland, Australia. In 2010, Grillo Mikrut organized the international Work-in-Progress postgraduate conference at the University of Queensland.

Anna Iatsenko holds a *Licence ès Lettres* in English, General Linguistics and Comparative Literature and an MA in English literature from the University of Geneva. She is currently completing a doctoral thesis on the relationship between music and language in Toni Morrison's fiction and occupies a position of teaching assistant.

Aoi Mori is a Professor of English at Meijigakuin University. She received her Ph.D. in English from State University of New York, Buffalo. In 2004, she spent a sabbatical year in African American Studies at Princeton University. She is the author of several books including *Toni Morrison and Womanist Discourse*.

Lynn Penrod is Professor of French in the Department of Modern Languages & Cultural Studies at the University of Alberta in Edmonton, Alberta, Canada. Her research and teaching focus on francophone women writers (Hélène Cixous, Simone de Beauvoir, George Sand), translation studies, French children's literature, and the interrelationship between law and literature. Dr Penrod is also a barrister & solicitor and lectures in the Faculty of Law. She is the author of five books and numerous scholarly articles and is a former President of the Social Sciences and Humanities Research Council of Canada. Her most recent publications are an article on using law as an approach to teaching George Sand's *Indiana*, an article on translation of contemporary French women writers, and an essay on Dany Laferrière's trilogy for children. She is in the final stages of completing the English translation of Hélène Cixous's *La fiancée juive*.

Sangita Rayamajhi, PhD, is a Professor at the Asian University for Women, an American University in Bangladesh. She teaches western and non-western fictions, gender and sexuality, and theater. Recently she has co-authored a book *Roles of Women in Asia*, published by Greenwood. She is the recipient of National Endowment for the Humanities (NEH) Fellowship, Fulbright Scholarship and Scholar Rescue Fund Fellowship (SRF).

Kerstin Shands is Professor of English at Södertörn University, Stockholm. Among her publications are *The Repair of the World: The Novels of Marge Piercy*, *Embracing Space: Spatial Metaphors in Feminist Discourse*, *Collusion and Resistance: Women Writing in English* (editor), and *Neither East Nor West: Postcolonial Essays on Literature, Culture and Religion* (editor).

Andrea Sillis is currently a PhD student at the University of Central Lancashire, UK, having previously taken a BA in Russian and Philosophy at

Keele University, UK, and an MA in Critical Theory and Modern Fiction at Exeter University, UK.

Tuire Valkeakari is Associate Professor of English at Providence College, Rhode Island, USA. She is the author of *Religious Idiom and the African American Novel, 1952–1998* (UP of Florida, 2007). Her articles have appeared in *Studies in American Fiction, Crossings, Atlantic Literary Review,* and *Atlantis.*

English Studies

1. Kerstin W. Shands (ed.), *Collusion and Resistance: Women Writing in English*, 2002
2. Kerstin W. Shands et al. (eds.), *Notions of America: Swedish Perspectives*, 2004
3. Kerstin W. Shands (ed.), *Neither East Nor West: Postcolonial Essays on Literature, Culture and Religion*, 2008
4. Kerstin W. Shands & Giulia Grillo Mikrut (eds), *Living Language, Living Memory: Essays on the Works of Toni Morrison*, 2014

www.ingramcontent.com/pod-product-compliance
Lightning Source LLC
Chambersburg PA
CBHW020657260626
47157CB00008B/3066